Deadly Vows

Books by Jody Holford

DEADLY NEWS

DEADLY VOWS

Published by Kensington Publishing Corporation

Deadly Vows

A Britton Bay Cozy Mystery

Jody Holford

LYRICAL UNDERGROUND
Kensington Publishing Corp.
www.kensingtonbooks.com

LYRICAL UNDERGROUND BOOKS are published by

Kensington Publishing Corp.
119 West 40th Street
New York, NY 10018

All Kensington titles, imprints, and distributed lines are available at special quantity discounts for bulk purchases for sales promotion, premiums, fund-raising, educational, or institutional use.

Special book excerpts or customized printings can also be created to fit specific needs. For details, write or phone the office of the Kensington Sales Manager: Kensington Publishing Corp., 119 West 40th Street, New York, NY 10018. Attn. Sales Department. Phone: 1-800-221-2647.

Lyrical Underground and Lyrical Underground logo Reg. US Pat. & TM Off.

First Electronic Edition: April 2019
ISBN-13: 978-1-5161-0867-1 (ebook)
ISBN-10: 1-5161-0867-1 (ebook)

First Print Edition: April 2019
ISBN-13: 978-1-5161-0870-1
ISBN-10: 1-5161-0870-1

Printed in the United States of America

And if love be madness; may I never find sanity again.
—John Mark Green

Chapter One

Watching the setup of a wedding was somewhat like going backstage at a play: it wrecked the magic. Or maybe, Molly Owens thought, as she sipped her delicious dark roast and leaned against the doorframe of her little cottage, it was the screeching bride-to-be putting a damper on the mood.

Tigger, the sweet black-and-white border collie she'd adopted quite by accident, growled and gave a little yip as he plopped his bottom on Molly's slipper.

"I know, buddy. Let's just assume she's stressed."

Glancing at her watch, Molly gave herself five more minutes of shameless observation. She was a people watcher by nature, which came in handy considering her job editing and sometimes writing the news. Even if she wasn't an avid fan of watching the interactions of people, she'd have been caught up in the palpable drama going on in the driveway of the bed-and-breakfast where she rented an adorable fairy-like home. The sprawling Victorian structure had been converted to a bed-and-breakfast years ago and, since Molly's arrival in Britton Bay only a few of months ago, never seemed to have a dull moment.

Currently, the blonde bride-to-be was yelling at one of the workers, seemingly not intimidated that he towered over her. Though her arm motions spoke louder than her words, Molly heard bits and pieces; words like "late" and "reliable." Seeing as the wedding party had only just arrived, Molly wondered what time the bride had expected the work crews. She knew the owner had been working round the clock to prepare for having a full house and a big event. Surely the bride didn't think the venue would be entirely ready to go when she arrived.

Even if she had thought the staging would be set, there was no way to ignore the beauty of her surroundings. Even without the trimmings of a wedding, the lot, the house, and the gardens were majestic.

Molly's cottage was set back on the large property, away from the main house and surrounded by trees and pretty flower beds. It was the perfect backdrop for the wedding scheduled for five days from now. Providing the bride didn't go into cardiac arrest before that.

Katherine Alderich, owner of the bed-and-breakfast, appeared as if out of nowhere. In reality, she'd likely come through the kitchen out onto the back deck and into the driveway. She spoke quietly to the bride and even from a distance Molly could see the kind glance she gave the chastised worker, who went back to carting tables and chairs from the truck to the yard.

Standing in front of the blonde, Katherine reminded Molly of a young Hepburn-esque actress giving a pep talk. Whatever she said had the bride nodding her head and then leaning in for a hug. Katherine put an arm around the woman, who looked a little younger than Molly's twenty-eight, and guided her toward the back deck. The sweet, mothering owner of the B and B had a way with words that usually stole an argument right out of the other person's mouth.

Molly pulled her phone out of her back pocket, her grin wide. Setting her coffee on the little table just inside her entrance way, she texted her boyfriend.

> *Your mom is a miracle worker. Still, I think the*
> *next five days are going to be stressful.*

Sam's response was almost instantaneous.

> *She does have a way about her. Getting a good*
> *view of all the happenings?*

Molly grinned, looking up to see another vehicle—a dark minivan— pulling into the drive.

> *And then some. I'm just about to leave for work.*
> *Hope you have a good day.*

> *It'd be better if I knew I'd see you later.*

Molly's heart double-jumped.

That could be arranged.

I'll bring dinner. We can pull your little bistro
table to the front yard and watch the show ;)

She laughed, thinking that even though they'd only been dating just shy of a couple of months, he knew her very well.

Sounds perfect. xo

* * * *

Despite the still early hour, by the time Molly left for work, the sun was on its way to burning up the concrete. Britton Bay, the seaside town she now called home, was getting a late summer heat wave. Sweat dripped down the curve of her back and she pictured jumping into her Jeep—roof off—just to speed up the journey. If she'd been on her own, she likely would have, but Tigger needed to expend some energy if he was going to hang around the newspaper office with Molly and her staff. He'd become something of a mascot and was well loved by everyone there. As she strolled along the sidewalk, nodding hello to tourists who were out for early morning fun at the beach, she breathed in the salty, sweet air. Maybe she'd see if Sam wanted to swim later. Or just hang out on the sand and watch the sun set over the ocean. Funny how she'd lived in LA for a long time and had never made use of the many beaches. But Britton Bay was literally a beachside town, unlike Lancaster, where she'd moved from. The easy access made a walk on the beach or a quick dip in the ocean easy to build into her routine.

Extending like long, winding arms from the beach were the two sides of Main Street. There was a host of different establishments offering tourists their heart's delight, be it milkshakes, confectionaries, or the best burgers south of Oregon. Along with those businesses, there was a pet food store, a small five and dime grocer, a spa-slash-hair-slash-gossip-salon, and her boyfriend's auto garage. There were few needs that couldn't be met in the central hub of town. The prices at the Main Street stores tended to be a little higher, given the traffic they received, but that changed with the coming and going of the seasons. This would be Molly's first shift from peak season into the quiet winter months.

Checking her watch once more, she decided she had enough time to stop in at Morning Muffins. Bella Reid was a genius with flour and sugar.

Molly's stomach growled just thinking about the lemon blueberry scones the baker had recently perfected.

"Hey Molly," Hannah Benedict, her boss's niece and one of their employees at the paper said.

Molly turned to see the teen walking toward her, looking like sunshine in a pair of capris and a flower patterned tank top. At seventeen, she was more mature than some of the adults Molly had met. There were times she forgot she was conversing with a teen, but then she'd see her like this, with her blonde hair pulled to the side in a thick braid, not a hint of makeup on her youthful face, and she'd remember how young she was. It seemed forever ago that Molly was the same age. *You didn't have it half as together as Hannah does.*

"Hey, Hannah. You're out and about early. I didn't think you were on at the paper until noon today."

Hannah crouched to greet Tigger, who acted as though he hadn't seen the girl in a month of Sundays. In reality, he'd seen her yesterday at the office.

"Yeah, I slept at my friend Dee's last night and wanted to go home before work. Hello to you, too. You're so cute. Yes, you are," Hannah said, laughing at the dog's enthusiasm. She looked up at Molly, her eyes squinting against the sun. "I still can't believe no one has claimed him."

Molly's heart squeezed painfully at the thought that anyone would. When she'd first found the little guy behind the newspaper offices, she'd been prepared to find his owner and even gave it a good try. But now, it had been almost a couple of months and she was more than a little attached. He was hers.

"Me neither, but Sam said there'd been a problem a while back with puppy mills so maybe he really doesn't have a home."

Hannah stood, brushed off her pants. Molly hadn't quite gotten Tigger to stop jumping yet.

"He does now," Hannah said.

Looking down at the adorable pup, Molly nodded. "Yeah, he does."

"You getting muffins?" Hannah gestured toward the bakery.

"I am. I'll buy you one if you hang on to Tigger for me."

Hannah held out her hand for the leash. "Deal. Chocolate chip, please."

Inside the shop was quiet. A couple of older ladies were chatting over large mugs of coffee and cinnamon buns at a table near the window. Bella was behind the counter, her hair tucked up in a high bun, her dark apron dusted with flour.

She glanced over and gave Molly about half the smile she gave most. "Morning, Molly."

"Good morning. It's quiet in here," Molly remarked. Bella was well-known by locals and tourists alike for her delicious treats.

"You just missed the rush actually. I think a lot of tourists are heading home so there was an early morning crowd."

Molly looked at the display case to see what was available. "You can't blame them for wanting one last taste." Her mouth watered.

Bella's smile morphed into the real thing. Molly was taking it one step at a time, trying to regain Bella's trust after mistakenly accusing the baker's boyfriend of foul play earlier in the summer.

She wiped her hands on her apron. "Thank you. What can I get you?"

If she thought too hard about it, she'd change her mind a dozen times. "I'll have a lemon blueberry scone and six chocolate chip muffins."

Bella laughed. "Hungry?"

Molly nodded her head toward the door where Hannah could be seen through the glass playing with the pup. "Might as well treat the staff."

"Good call." Bella got a box for Molly's order and slid open the case. "So, how's the B and B? The wedding is this weekend, right?"

News moved through Britton Bay quicker than Tigger gobbled his food. The wedding was worthy of big-time gossip among the locals since the mother of the bride had grown up in the converted Victorian. The childhood connection had warmed Katherine's heart, making her agree to host the entire wedding party in the six rooms she had available.

Molly leaned on the counter while Bella grabbed the muffins. "It is. They started arriving this morning. Loudly."

Bella taped the box shut and glanced at Molly, one eyebrow arched. "Uh-oh. My mom went to school with the bride's mom. Said she was quite the diva. Of course, she could have just been trying to make me feel better after Katherine called me about the catering."

Bagging up the scone and passing it over, Bella rang up the order. Molly tried to think of a polite way to quell her curiosity as she tapped in her PIN.

"What happened with the catering?" There was no polite way to be nosy.

The baker huffed out a breath and pushed a strand of hair off her forehead with the back of her hand. "You know I normally supply Katherine's baked goods and she'd explained to the mother of the bride that breakfasts were included, but she insisted that they wanted their own caterer even for the days before the wedding."

Molly accepted the bag from Bella after tucking her bank card away. "Hmm. They do strike me as the types to be quite particular."

When a timer dinged, Bella glanced toward the door of the kitchen, then back at Molly. "I'll say. Apparently the caterer won some big culinary contest and they wanted the wedding party to experience the award-winning delights for all five days."

Though there was a tinge of irritation in the baker's voice, she didn't seem angry about the loss of income. Molly knew, firsthand, that it was in Bella's nature to forgive and forget. Mostly. Despite her apology for adding Callan, the shake shop owner, and Bella's guy to her list of suspects who may have wanted her former colleague dead, there was still a certain amount of stiffness to the interactions she had with the baker. Molly's not so polite nosiness had created potholes in the road to friendship with Bella. Plus, she'd been completely wrong. Molly was still hoping things would feel natural between them since they were close in age and she genuinely liked the baker.

"Well, I don't care if she was given an award by Gordon Ramsey himself, there's no way whatever caterer they're bringing could make better muffins or scones than you."

Bella smiled, all traces of tension vanishing from the woman's features. Her dark brown eyes showed a mixture of affection and appreciation, making Molly grateful she kept trying to iron things out.

"Thanks. I better go or the next batch of scones will be anything but award worthy."

Molly waved and went back out to greet Hannah and her Tigger. The dog jumped and yipped with unadulterated glee and Molly laughed, trading Hannah the leash for the box of muffins.

"Mind carrying those?" The *Britton Bay Bulletin*'s office was on the way to Hannah's so Molly assumed the girl would walk with her and the dog.

As expected, Hannah took the box and fell into step beside her.

"So, I was thinking we could do a story about the wedding. Well, the bed-and-breakfast really. We could feature the house, which would give Katherine more exposure right?"

Molly couldn't hold back the wattage on her smile. Hannah was a bright girl with an excellent talent for storytelling. She interned at the paper in between classes during the school year, but had been working close to full time all summer. As usual, her idea was bright and fun and relevant. Something the newspaper had been missing when Molly arrived in town.

"It absolutely would and I agree, there's a ton we could do surrounding the wedding. It's important to have stories that pique interest," Molly agreed as she thought about what Bella said.

As they neared the office, she added, "And I'm pretty sure there's plenty of people interested in seeing how this wedding plays out."

Chapter Two

The building that housed the newspaper office sat at the end of Main Street. A right or left turn led to residential neighborhoods with a mix of duplexes, cottage style homes, and a few apartment complexes.

Even though Molly had moved from a suburb in California, the vibe in this one was far calmer than any she'd ever known. It was like just being in Britton Bay slowed her pulse and forced her to move at a less frantic pace. It tried to, anyway. Molly liked to be busy and on the go.

This made her multipurpose position at the *Britton Bay Bulletin* very fulfilling. Letting herself in through the back door, she waited until it shut behind her to walk through the small alcove that led to the main areas. She headed for the kitchen to put the muffins on a plate and grab herself some coffee. Though she could hear music and a bit of chatter, no one else was in the kitchen. Flipping on the light, she grabbed a plate and cup. Hannah had taken Tigger home with her and would bring him back when she came to work.

"Mmm, what's in the box?" Elizabeth asked, joining Molly at the counter, her mug empty.

"Muffins. Help yourself," Molly said, giving the woman a smile.

Elizabeth had been a writer for the paper for many years and was good friends with the owner and his wife. From the beginning, she'd welcomed Molly with open arms. And at the time, Molly had desperately needed all the people in her corner that she could get. Being the new girl and getting put in charge didn't always make someone the favorite among the other staff.

"You're such a doll. How's it going? The wedding extravaganza starts today, right?" Elizabeth grabbed some milk from the apartment size fridge.

"Already started. They were unloading canopies, tables and chairs when I left."

"Katherine is a saint. I know she's used to tourists, but to have that many in your house for that many days would make me crazy. Especially..." Elizabeth's voice trailed off and Molly looked her way, taking a sip of her coffee before it was cool enough to do so.

"Especially?"

A pinkish hue colored the attractive woman's cheeks. In her late fifties, Elizabeth had both a reserved elegance and youthful grace that drew people in. Much like Molly's landlord.

"No. Forget I said anything. She's coming in today to provide some photographs that we're running in tomorrow's edition," Elizabeth said.

Curiosity tickled at the base of her skull, but Molly simply nodded and let it go.

"Yes. I've saved space in the layout. Is everyone else here? I'd like to do a quick meeting about the extra edition this week."

On top of commandeering the bed-and-breakfast, the bridal party—or more specifically, the mother of the bride—had made the rounds and asked particular local businesses to take part in celebrating her daughter; mostly the newspaper, the hotel, and the marina.

"I'll let everyone know," Elizabeth said, walking out of the kitchen.

The floorplan of the newspaper headquarters reminded Molly of one of those miniature architectural models; a bunch of squares attached to a central rectangle. The main rectangle housed the design counter, several desks with partitions, and an open area where Molly had a whiteboard installed for brainstorming sessions.

Off of this common area was Alan Benedict's office. Despite his family owning the newspaper for a couple of generations, her boss was approachable and down-to-earth. Molly had her own office, another little square, across the room from Alan's. There was a bathroom and utility room off of the kitchen. Downstairs housed the real hub of the entire building: the printing press.

Molly plated the muffins, intent on gathering her staff. She was pleased to see they were all waiting near the whiteboard, a couple of them on stools and the others standing chatting. She put the muffins on the waist height, wide countertop where they all worked on the layouts together.

"Good morning," Molly said.

She was greeted with a chorus of cheerful replies that she suspected were more for the muffins than her. She laughed when Jill Alderich, their newest staff writer—and Sam's cousin—beat Clay to one that had more chocolate chips. Molly hadn't been a fan of the twentysomething social media coordinator slash photographer when she'd met him. After finding Clay's father dead in his apartment, Molly's guilt had pushed her to dig into the death of their former features writer. Through that ordeal, she'd come to see Clay in a new light. Or at least, a less annoying one.

"Cheater," Clay said, winking at Jill.

Jill rolled her eyes. "All's fair in love and muffins."

"How are you today, Molly?" Alan asked, breaking a muffin apart.

"I'm good thanks. Excited about this week. I think we have a lot of avenues to take with the wedding and the exposure it'll give the surrounding businesses."

Alan nodded. "I agree—"

His sentence was cut short when the front door of the *Britton Bay Bulletin* pushed open. Two women Molly didn't recognize walked in talking so quickly and loudly that everyone else turned to stare.

Just before the first woman, whose bleached blonde ponytail bounced with every step, spoke, Alan groaned.

"Oh, Alan! Look at you! You've aged so well," the woman said, hurrying forward and wrapping her arms around him.

Molly arched an eyebrow at Elizabeth then looked back at Alan who patted the woman's back stiffly.

He put his hands on her arms and pushed her away gently. "How are you Patty?"

Ahhh, Patty, as in Patricia Lovenly, aka mother of the bride.

"I'm wonderful. I mean, I'm stressed and emotional, but I'm absolutely fabulous. I'm so excited to be *home*."

"Yes, I'm sure. We're all excited to have you here, too. The town is buzzing with excitement over your daughter's wedding."

The woman who'd accompanied Patty stared down at the watch that took up a good amount of space on her wrist.

"As it should be," Patty said, swatting Alan's chest.

Both of Molly's eyebrows itched to bounce up. Elizabeth covered her mouth, presumably to hide a smirk.

"This might breathe a little life back into this sleepy little town, even temporarily."

As if bored of the show, the second woman looked up and cleared her throat. "I'd like to get to the hotel and change before meeting with my staff," she said.

Her angular face reminded Molly of a triangle. With blonde pixie cut hair, she was attractive, probably a bit younger than Molly's twenty-eight, but the harsh lines of her face and the way she scowled shadowed any positive features.

Patty turned and clapped her hands together. "Right. Of course. I'm so sorry. Alan, this is Skyler Friessen. She's the celebrity chef who will be catering my Chantel's wedding. I was just taking her to her hotel and then back to the bed-and-breakfast. Just picked her up from the airport and thought I'd do everything in one trip. I have the photos for the newspaper spread."

Patty dug through her oversized bag and pulled out an envelope. Skyler shoved her hands in the pockets of her black chinos and glanced around the office. Molly thought about what Bella had told her this morning. "Welcome to Britton Bay. I've heard wonderful things about your cooking," Molly said. She held out her hand. "I'm Molly Owens, editor here at the *Britton Bay Bulletin.*"

The look on the woman's face could only be described as haughty. Straightening her shoulders, she elongated her neck as though that would better allow her to look down on Molly.

"Cooking? I prefer to call it creating. I'm an artist. My medium is food. Though, this is actually my last event of this type. I'm opening my own restaurant."

Patty beamed. "What a way to go out. The wedding of the century."

Elizabeth's eyes widened at the exaggeration; they were hardly the royal family. Molly smiled then pressed her lips inward, unsure of what to say. Thinking about the possibilities for the newspaper and remembering something else, Molly held up a hand.

"You won a contest, didn't you?" That was what Bella had said.

The chef's smile slipped. "My work was recognized for its Michelin star worthy taste, yes."

"It was a local contest?" Molly figured they could do a small feature on the chef since they were covering the wedding anyway. Everyone would be curious since only a handful of people from the town had been invited.

"My hometown, yes. The contest is irrelevant," Skyler said, looking at the square screen on her smart watch. She swiped the screen and tapped on it.

Jill and Clay drifted to their desks, no doubt eager to bury their heads in anything but the tension buzzing in the small circle.

Molly's skin prickled. "Wasn't the contest the launching point for your award-winning status?"

Skyler's neck snapped up and her gaze all but scorched Molly. "Some things are bound to happen regardless. When someone is destined to shine, they will. With or without *irrelevant* little contests."

Patty's smile slipped and she looked back and forth between Molly and Skyler. "Oh, well, yes, that was just one accomplishment in a long list of them. Anyway, I'll leave these pictures with you, Alan. I need to get Skyler settled in at the hotel."

"You're not staying at the bed-and-breakfast?" Alan asked, accepting the photos.

Skyler glanced at Alan through lowered lashes, still typing on her watch. "No. The wedding party is taking all of the rooms. That definitely would have been more convenient." She paused and gave Patty a look that Molly was grateful she wasn't on the receiving end of, then continued, "I'm meeting my staff there this afternoon, but we're all staying in the local hotel. Which I'm hoping has modern day amenities."

Patty's face paled. Elizabeth stepped closer. "I think you'll find the hotel has everything you need. Though we're a small town, we came into the twenty-first century along with everyone else," Elizabeth said, her tone suspiciously sweet. Then she pointed at Skyler's watch. "You could probably even look that up on your little watch there."

Alan put a hand on Patty's shoulder and stepped forward. "Well, it was lovely of you to drop by. We should all get back to work. Thanks for bringing these photos in. Skyler, it was a pleasure to meet you."

He all but shoved them out the door. Molly stared through the wide picture window that looked out on Main Street. Patty said something to Skyler, but the chef just continued walking to the passenger side of an SUV. She opened the door and slid in.

"Those people are horrible," Elizabeth said.

Molly shook her head. "Good for you for putting her in her place. I doubt your words will keep her there though. Wow."

Jill whistled and leaned back in her chair. "I think we should do a pool. The wedding extravaganza lasts five days. I'm betting there's a fight before Friday."

Clay laughed and pulled out his wallet. "I say someone has one tomorrow."

It was only Wednesday, but so far, Molly had seen enough to think it might not even take that long. She kept quiet.

"Knock it off. No betting. Molly, sorry about that. Patty always was a little...high maintenance." Alan grinned as he spoke, but looked a tad exasperated.

"No reason to apologize. The chef has quite the chip on her shoulder."

"Fame does that to some people," Elizabeth said, picking up a muffin and taking it to her desk.

"She's hardly famous. She won a culinary cook-off on a cable channel. Her recipe was printed in a food magazine and she won a chunk of prize money. Award or no award, like most restaurants, hers will probably close within a year of opening," Jill said.

Molly sipped her coffee, her brain swirling. It wasn't even noon yet and she felt like there were enough stories simmering in Britton Bay to fuel a month of papers.

"You know a lot about her," she said.

Jill shrugged and opened her laptop. "I like research. Plus, I was there when Bella got a call from Katherine saying her baked goods wouldn't be needed for a week. Bella was really…insulted. She got it and I don't think she blamed my aunt, but I think it hurt her feelings."

"I spoke to Bella this morning, too. She seemed okay with it." But maybe she wasn't. Maybe she was irritated to be shut out of an event that could have boosted her business. She wasn't the only food service in town that had been nixed. The owners of the popular hot spot, Come 'n Get It Eatery, had offered to host the rehearsal dinner and had been shot down as well.

Only the best for Chantel Lovenly.

"I don't know. Maybe she's a great chef, but I can't see any baked goods topping Bella's. Plus, Bella is hot. That chick was snotty looking," Clay said, typing something on his keyboard.

Alan groaned and Molly rolled her eyes.

"Very thorough assessment, Clay. I'd say Jill could safely bet on you not doing any writing for the paper anytime soon."

The others, including Clay, laughed. Molly went to her office, her thoughts on the wedding and the chaos that would descend in close quarters over the next several days. She'd have a front row seat to what promised to be an entertaining event.

Pulling her own laptop out of her bag, she booted it up. Maybe it wouldn't be a bad idea to get to know some of the players. In the age of Facebook and other social media, a few clicks on the keyboard would give her some insight into the people staying mere steps away from her cottage. Instead of looking up Patty or Chantel however, Molly typed in Skyler's name. If she could get some background information on the chef and her assent to so-called fame, maybe Molly could convince her to do an interview. If she had as much cachet as her body language and attitude suggested, the paper's reach could extend much further than Britton Bay.

Molly smiled at the list of results that showed up on her screen. She wouldn't be the only person to write about Skyler Friessen that was for sure. *So, find a completely fresh angle.* Molly had a feeling it was the only way the woman would even agree to be questioned. While her food was said to be "bold, fresh, and delightful", Molly had just seen that the same could not be said about Skyler. She'd have to appeal to her vanity. Which meant finding an in.

Chapter Three

By the time Molly got home that evening, her stomach was growling. Other than the scone and a muffin, she hadn't stopped to eat. Tigger was pulling on his leash, eager to explore every scent available. He stopped at one of the two rose bushes that flanked the cobblestone walk at the front of the bed-and-breakfast. There was a little path off of this one that led to her cabin.

The yard had been transformed into a tented ballroom during the day. There was an elevated dance floor with a couple of steps leading up to it. People Molly didn't recognize were still working on centerpieces, decorations, and organizing tables. *How much money do these people have?* Molly had never come close to getting married, but if the day did come, she'd like a smaller event. Much smaller. Though, she couldn't fault the choice of location.

"See something you like?" Sam asked from behind her.

Tigger went haywire, pulling on his leash. Molly let it go so the dog didn't strangle himself.

"I do now," Molly replied, still not used to the little skip her heart gave when she saw him. Every time.

Sam winked at her before he crouched down to greet Tigger. "That makes two of us. Hey, buddy. Okay, three of us. How you doing, pal? Okay, calm down. Yes, I've missed you, too."

Tigger rolled, belly up and gazed adoringly at Molly's boyfriend. *Can't really blame him.*

"Okay. That's enough. You got yours," Sam said, standing. He picked up the leash and closed the slight distance between him and Molly.

"My turn?" Molly asked, working hard not to copy the dog's adoring look.

Sam smirked, tugging gently on a strand of her hair. "Do you want me to rub your belly or will you settle for a kiss?"

She laughed and leaned into him, showing him her preference as she went up on tip toes to touch her mouth to his. The zap of electricity that whipped through her when they kissed hadn't lessened over the last couple of months. If anything, the buzz seemed to last longer and feel more charged.

She wasn't a cynic, but since she moved to Britton Bay after her live-in boyfriend brought one of his exes back to their place, it was harder to trust. Sam was working his way under her skin and into her heart with his effortless charm and kindness. His six foot two frame, dark hair, and gorgeous brown eyes didn't hurt either.

"I missed you," he said, pulling her into a hug. Tigger flopped down between their legs, unconcerned with any sort of personal space. The dog was like Velcro and as though he was afraid of being left behind, tended to stay as close as he could.

"Me, too," Molly admitted, resting her cheek against Sam's chest.

Around them, people chatted easily as the breeze blew the trees, sharing the scent of roses and other flowers Molly couldn't name.

Sam leaned back, which had Tigger sitting up, eager to take part in whatever was next. From the corner of her eye, Molly saw a group of six women, one being Chantel, the bride, laughing as they walked up the front steps that led to a wide porch. She wondered if the five women were all part of the bridal party.

"You want the good news or bad news?" Sam asked.

Molly's chest tightened. No one liked bad news. "Good?"

"I brought fried chicken, potato salad, and homemade biscuits from Come 'n Get It Eatery. Calli says you need to call her for a girls' night by the way."

Molly smiled. Calliope owned the very popular diner on Main Street and, like much of the town, had charmed Molly through and through. "That sounds delicious and I absolutely will. Bad news?"

Nothing bad. Nothing bad.

"My mom got ousted from her kitchen this evening so the wedding party could have a private tasting with the chef they brought. So I invited her to join us. Thought we could eat on her back deck?"

Molly released the breath that had caught in her lungs. "So, the bad news is we have to eat some of my favorite food with your mother, whom I adore. You can always give me bad news."

Sam chuckled and took her hand as they walked toward her cottage. "The bad news is we can't be alone."

She nudged him with her hip, digging her keys out of her bag. "It'll give your mom a break. I know this is what she does, but having this many people all at once and then being put out of your own space can't be easy."

Opening her front door, they stepped in. Molly took Tigger's leash off while Sam shut the door.

"She's more excited than anything. I do plan on hanging out more for the next several days, just in case she needs an extra set of hands. It looks like they have most things covered, but I know she won't be happy unless she's busy and I don't want her overdoing it."

Molly snorted quietly and slipped off her shoes in the small entryway, setting her bag down on the rectangular table she kept there. Katherine had as much energy and enthusiasm as Tigger. "Dare you to say that to your mom."

Sam laughed behind her. "No thanks."

The pretty daisies Molly had put in the ceramic vase she'd bought from a local potter were starting to wilt. She picked them up off the entry table, vase and all, looking back over her shoulder. "Was that meant to be more bad news?"

He followed her into the kitchen. "What's that?"

Leaving the flowers on the counter, she opened the fridge, took out two bottles of water and passed him one. She left hers on the counter so she could grab Tigger's bowl. "You'll be hanging around more than usual."

He snagged her wrist as she was slipping past him, with a grin that made his eyes crinkle.

"You're pretty funny," he said, stroking a hand down her hair with a look of affection that made her stomach flip-flop.

It was just the wedding and his good looks, his easy personality making her feel…dreamy. She poked him in the stomach teasingly. "It's a backup if editing news doesn't work out. Speaking of which, I met the mother of the bride today and the chef. I'd like to see if I can convince her to do an interview for the paper. So this could work out in my favor."

Grabbing Tigger's bowl, she headed to the sink, then added, "Other than not getting some time to ourselves, I mean."

Sam laughed and took the toy Tigger offered, hanging onto it so the dog could tug the other end.

"Uh-huh. Nice save." His phone buzzed and he took it out, glanced at it. "I've got to go up and help my mom grab a ladder from the garage then I'll set the food out. See you up there?"

She put Tigger's bowl down and came over to stand in front of him. Tigger trotted over to his water and took a noisy slurp.

"I'm going to change and then I'll be up," she said, stepping into him and wrapping her arms around his waist. "And also, I'm really glad you'll be around lots."

Being scared to open her heart didn't mean she couldn't return his generous affection, in both words and actions.

His squeeze and kiss on the top of her head warmed her from the inside out and made her want to hang on just a bit longer. Instead, she stepped back.

* * * *

When she took the path to the main house, Tigger on a leash at her side, she couldn't help but smile.

"It looks like a real life fairy tale," she told the dog. He didn't love the leash, but with all of the tents and chairs, she didn't want to chance him getting curious. Like her, it was in his nature.

A large picture window at the side of the house showed the guests laughing as they sat around Katherine's long, rustic dining table. Molly wondered what Ms. Skyler was preparing for the evening. Rounding the small bend beside the driveway, she saw Katherine and Sam already seated. As she approached, they both saw her and Sam stood, taking Tigger's leash when she came up the steps.

The back porch was much smaller than the front, but it was quaint with a patio table, chairs, and a couple of benches furnishing it. It was a perfect spot to sit and read the paper while drinking coffee. Since her arrival, Molly had ensured that the guests had the latest edition of the *Britton Bay Bulletin* available.

"There's my guy," Katherine said, patting her legs so Tigger would come to her.

He tripped over his paws on the way there, his tail doing a tornado-speed wag. Sam pulled Molly's chair out and pushed it in when she sat.

"You've certainly raised a gentleman, Katherine," Molly said, smiling at him then looking at Katherine.

"I should hope so," his mom replied.

Happy to just be near them, Tigger flopped down under the table while they passed the take-out containers of chicken, salad, and biscuits. A fresh pitcher of lemonade sat in the center of the table and Molly poured a glass for each of them.

There was a small window over the sink in the kitchen, but Molly didn't see anyone through it. She was hoping to run into Skyler at some point before the evening was over.

"How's it going in there?" Molly bit into her chicken, sighing in delight as she looked at Katherine.

"Good. They're probably the highest maintenance bunch I've had, but to be fair, weddings can be stressful and I've never had any big events here—other than milestone birthdays and such."

"You know the bride's mom, right?" Sam asked, a forkful of salad half-way to his mouth.

"I went to school with her. We weren't friends, but I remember walking by this house when she lived in it and thinking it was the prettiest one around."

Molly looked around, admiring the way the sun still clung to the sky, just over the wide expanse of trees. "It really is a perfect spot."

She already knew that Katherine had done several renovations to make some smaller rooms out of larger ones, add the backyard cottage, and spruce up the landscaping. She hired out for big jobs—or had Sam help her—but she was always working, always making it just a little bit…more.

Sam dropped a bite of his chicken on the porch and the scramble of paws was instantaneous. Molly narrowed her eyes at him, despite the innocent grin he flashed her.

"What? It slipped."

Katherine laughed. "A gentleman and a lousy liar."

"Hey," Sam protested, dropping another small bite.

"Enough. He'll get sick." She took another bite of chicken and the crispy buttermilk skin practically melted in her mouth. "Besides, it's a waste of amazing food. They should have just had Calliope and Dean cater."

Katherine leaned in. "Nothing small-town for Patty's daughter. Other than location I mean."

Sam licked his fingers, then picked up his napkin. "Small towns have the best kept secrets."

Molly looked at him, her heart doing that strange, tight-squeeze thing again. *They certainly do.* "What do the next few days look like?"

Tigger lay down on her foot, which kept her from tapping it on the deck.

Katherine wiped her mouth and glanced back at the kitchen. "I've been given an extensive itinerary so I can be very specific if you'd like, but to sum it up, there's a brunch tomorrow with some of Patty's family who still live in the area. The gals have a spa day planned after that, and the kitchen will be busy with the chef and her staff getting things ready. I guess they'll provide simple lunches and family style meals until the rehearsal dinner, which I've heard is going to be almost as fancy as the wedding. Sunday afternoon, everything gets taken down and I've got guests coming in on Tuesday."

Sam swallowed his last bite of food and frowned at his mom. "That's not a lot of turnaround time."

Katherine waved her fork at him. "Don't start with me. It's plenty." She looked at Molly, one brow arched. "He likes to pretend I'm old and feeble. Thinks I need a week in between guests just to make some beds."

Rolling his eyes, Sam crumpled his napkin and tossed it on his plate. "I just don't want you overdoing it. When you started this, it was a few guests a month. Now you're constantly booked solid. I think you should start bringing in some help for the turnaround days after long-term guests or a full house."

Molly gave Sam a supportive nod. They'd talked about this, as it had been weighing on his mind. She didn't have the same worries he did, but cleaning her tiny place took her half a day, so she could certainly see his concern with Katherine taking on a full house with barely a day in between. That didn't even include laundry and stocking up on provisions.

"I'll think about it," Katherine said, pushing her plate away.

Sam grinned like he won the lottery. "Really? That was easy."

Molly nudged him with her foot. "Best not to gloat."

Katherine laughed then looked down at her plate, which had Sam's lips tilting down.

"Mom?"

She looked at Sam and Molly felt like she should give them a minute. Before she could excuse herself, Katherine put her hand over Sam's on the table.

"It was easy because as much as I love doing this, I wouldn't mind having a few hours to myself now and again. Time to do something just for me. Get my nails done, see a movie. Go on a date."

Molly's eyes widened just as Sam's jaw dropped and he asked, "Excuse me? A date?"

Katherine sat back, removing her hand and stiffening her shoulders, giving Sam a look Molly imagined she had long ago when he'd said something naughty. "Yes. A date. I'm a grown woman and I'm entitled. Brandon has asked me several times now and I don't want to keep saying no."

Sam sat forward. "Brandon? Wait—the sheriff?"

Molly bit her lip. She could have predicted that. Through a series of unfortunate events, Molly had spent some time with the sheriff while she'd been caught in the middle of Clay's father's murder investigation. Vernon East had not been a nice man, but no one deserved that sort of end. The sheriff was kind and trustworthy and, when he thought no one was looking, completely enamored with Sam's mom.

"Uh, I'm just going to use the washroom. Okay if I use the one off of the kitchen or should I go down to my place?" Molly stood, putting her napkin on her plate.

Katherine glanced at her, still sitting stiffly with a frown on her face. "Use this one. I'm sure it's fine. Not like they're eating in the kitchen."

On her way by, Molly gave Sam's shoulder a squeeze. Tigger lifted his head, but put it back down when she told him to stay. Letting herself into the mudroom just off of the kitchen, she removed her shoes and stepped into the kitchen.

Skyler was standing, alone, with her head bowed and her hands gripping the counter. The scents were incredible—herbs and spices, and something sweet. It almost made Molly forget she was full. Giving Sam and his mom a minute had worked out perfectly.

Skyler turned and looked at her and before Molly could say anything, the chef pointed at her and asked, "What the hell are you doing here?"

Chapter Four

Molly froze and almost looked behind her to make sure Skyler was, in fact, addressing her. The chef snarled and stalked toward her, quick enough that Molly stepped back, coming up against the door.

"I'm going to use the washroom," she said, hooking her thumb toward the door and thinking quickly. "I was having dinner with my boyfriend and his mom, Katherine."

Skyler stopped about a foot from Molly. Loud laughter floated in from the dining area. The angry creases in the corners of her eyes smoothed.

"You're a reporter. You just happen to be dining *here*?" She shoved her hands in the pockets of her black chef pants. Her hair was pulled away from her face with a thin, tight headband and with the unhappy set of her jaw, the chef looked even more severe than this morning.

"You're forgetting you're in a small town. I live in the cottage on the property. I'm dating Katherine Alderich's son. She lives here. We're having dinner."

Molly wasn't a reporter but at the moment, she wanted to know why that would have made the chef so mad.

Some of the stiffness fell from the woman's shoulders and she lost the edge on her expression. Her face was neutral, but compared to her scowl, it made her almost approachable. Molly wondered if the pressure of this event or what came after it was responsible for the bags under the chef's eyes.

"Also, I'm an editor for a small-town paper. Not a reporter. Huge difference there."

"Well, you can understand why I'd make the mistake. I'm tired of people asking me how I feel about winning and what if was like to win prize money. I just want to cook."

If that was Skyler's version of an apology, Molly sincerely hoped she was better at cooking. The door leading to the dining area pushed open and two people—one woman and one man—in aprons walked in, smiling and chatting. They froze, staring at Molly and Skyler, the door swinging behind them. Skyler's shoulders tightened again and her scowl reappeared. She turned and glared at them.

"Done socializing? About time. The next round is ready to go. Lucky for you it's a cold plate or it'd be ruined."

These people were not children, yet they each looked as if they'd been scolded by their parent. The guy stared at Skyler a moment, his eyes intense and she shifted, but didn't say a word, just held his gaze. The woman frowned and Molly thought she saw a flash of anger in the flare of her nostrils and the set of her eyes, but she schooled it and turned away. In unison, both the man and the woman muttered apologies as they moved to the food and each took what they could hold, which was an impressive four plates each. Molly had tried waitressing for exactly half a day before realizing she'd spend more money replacing dishes than she'd earn.

Turning back to her, Skyler's eyes went to the door. "Aren't they waiting for you?"

She wasn't going to get another chance to ask and the very worst she could say was no. Molly had heard no before. She could live with it. *Okay, she could probably do a little worse than no since she's staring daggers your way.*

"It must be hard to have so many people coming at you when all you want to do is cook."

Surprise widened Skyler's light-colored eyes. "It is. I'm pulled in a dozen different directions. The distractions impact my cooking." Hooking a thumb over her shoulder, she added, "Right now it's just my sous chefs, but for the wedding there'll be a dozen servers in the way as well." Some might look forward to the many hands assisting them, but Skyler was clearly not one of them.

Molly leaned against the counter in a hopefully casually stance. "I'm not a reporter, but I do write articles. I'd love to do something unique on you, Skyler. Maybe something about how you both fuel yourself and provide for others through your creations."

Skyler's brow arched. "What's in it for you?"

Molly wasn't taking the bait on that one. It could be absolutely nothing in it for her. "Finding the oyster."

The chef scowled. "Excuse me?" Her tone nearly as sharp as a knife.

Molly straightened. All or nothing. "I'm offering a peek at the woman underneath. Inside the shell so to speak. You're clearly passionate about your cooking. What does it do for you? What does it give you? How does it help you give back? Those are the things you want people to understand."

The frown slipped so Molly pressed the advantage. "I read a number of articles and interviews about your success and who you want to emulate. As you said, there was a lot of focus on the prize money and your win. I'd like to do an interview that focuses on what makes you unique and cutting edge in the culinary industry. If you're interested. If not, no hard feelings."

The sous chefs, who were doubling as waiters, returned as Skyler continued to stare at Molly. The woman's eyes roamed over both Skyler and Molly. Her ponytail seemed far too high to be comfortable. Dressed like the guy, she wore a crisp white shirt, buttoned to the neck and a pair of black pants. Her gaze bounced back and forth between Molly and the chef. "Everything all right?"

Skyler turned her head. "Any reason it shouldn't be?"

The woman's eyes narrowed slightly. "You just seem tense and since tonight is only a sample of some of the dishes and it's going well, I wondered why."

Good question. She isn't even in the middle of preparing anything and she's strung tighter than the sous chef's ponytail.

"Just because tonight isn't full of pressure, doesn't mean we can rest easy."

The woman nodded. "Sorry for asking." Molly couldn't help but think the woman often was—sorry for asking her boss anything.

Skyler gave an exasperated sigh. "Fine. We need baked goods for the morning. Apparently I'm a damn pastry chef now, too."

"They did offer to bring in the baking," the woman said in a low voice, her eyes averted.

Skyler turned her entire body in the woman's direction and waited until her sous chef raised her head and met her gaze. "My kitchen, my rules. If you don't like it, you're free to go."

The other cook nodded and got to work, while Skyler returned her unfriendly gaze to Molly, who felt the need to back up in the suddenly cramped space. It seemed impossible to her that a grown woman would let someone speak to her in that tone, with that level of disdain. It was one thing to have a grouchy boss, but Skyler took that to a whole new level. She started to tell the woman to never mind the interview because she wasn't all that sure she wanted to spend more time in her presence.

Skyler huffed out a breath. "Drop by my hotel room tomorrow morning. Around eight. Twenty minutes is all I can spare so you'd better have your questions ready."

Finished with the conversation, she turned her back and went to the counter. *Okay then.* Something about what she'd said—maybe the way she'd appealed to the woman's vanity—had worked in her favor and Molly was too excited to let the dismissal bother her. She turned and headed out the door back to Sam and his mom.

They'd settled their difference of opinion by the time Molly returned, her smile impossible to hide.

"Uh-oh," Sam said, grinning back at her. "You have that look."

He knew her looks? "What look? I don't have looks."

Katherine laughed. "Oh, yes, you do. And this one says, I got exactly what I wanted."

Molly's head whipped in Katherine's direction. *She* knew her looks, *too.* "You two are sneaky."

She sat down and Sam took her hand. "Because we can read you?"

The thought that they could—that *he* could—both unnerved and centered her. As an army brat, she'd been used to short-term friendships. In California, the place she'd previously settled the longest, she'd had lots of acquaintances, but only one close *friend.* Thinking of Tori made her miss her best friend.

Molly had moved to Britton Bay intending to put down roots, make a life for herself. And while she didn't think she had trust issues, she was quickly realizing that building that life would include lowering her walls and letting people in. For so many years, the only person she'd let in was Tori. Even with her ex—she'd been waiting for the other shoe to drop and hadn't even been surprised when it ended. Molly looked at Sam. She'd feel more sadness if something happened to their relationship than she had been over the break-up that brought her here.

"You okay?" He leaned in so their faces were closer, giving them the illusion of privacy.

"Yes," she said, nodding and tightening her fingers around his. "I'm good. And you're both right. I got Skyler to agree to an interview."

"Skyler?"

"She's the chef," Katherine said. "Very good, from what I hear. I was hoping to sample a bit in passing, but from what I've seen, she runs a pretty tight—non-sampling—kitchen. No sampling, no outside ingredients. They're only supposed to be here until about eight tonight. Then they're back in the morning."

Sam glanced to the door then back at the women. "She's just a cook. Do they really think their wedding is better because they found someone with a flashy reputation?"

Molly shrugged. Appearances mattered to a lot of people. "I get the feeling it does matter to them, particularly the mom. But not having decent food wouldn't be a great memory of your wedding."

Sam smiled at her quietly—mostly with his eyes. "No. But there are plenty of ways to have excellent food and even an amazing celebration without…" He gestured to the house. "All of this."

"Your father and I were married at the ocean. It was wonderful. Just us, our families, and some close friends. I don't even remember the food."

Molly smiled when Sam reached out and rubbed his hand over his mom's arm. They'd lost Sam's dad years ago. From the stories she'd heard, he'd left quite a void.

Katherine's eyes took on a faraway look for a moment and then she smiled like she was reminding herself to do so. "You two should go enjoy the rest of your evening. I'll clean this up."

"We can help, Mom." Sam stood and Molly followed.

"It'll give me something to do. Off you go. Why don't you take Molly down to the beach?" She stood to collect the dishes. "It's your first end of season. You need to check out Britton Bay's Sidewalk Celebration."

Molly knew that several local and visiting vendors were set up along the sidewalk that ran between the beach and its parking lot. They'd run some articles about it in the paper, but Jill had covered them, taking pictures and interviewing some of the people planning to sell their arts, crafts, and foods. Back in town after being away, Sam's cousin was eager to throw herself into her new job and reconnect with old friends and acquaintances. As the editor, Molly worked behind the scenes, unless they were short-staffed or working on something special.

"Do you want to go?" Sam asked. He grinned at her. "There'll be music and food samples."

It would be a shame to miss something that was clearly another small piece of Britton Bay's traditions.

Molly looked at Katherine, hesitant to leave the woman alone with her sad thoughts. "Why don't you come with us?"

She waved Molly's suggestion away with her free hand. "No, no. I need to be here in case anyone needs anything. I'll see you both tomorrow. Thank you for a lovely meal and the company."

It was a much politer dismissal than the one Molly had received from Skyler, but there was a hint of loneliness in it. Sam leaned into his mom and kissed her cheek. The quiet melancholy shifting Katherine's mood prompted Molly to give her a tight hug before taking Sam's hand. They walked back to the cottage in the deep dusk, the serene sound of evening enveloping them.

"I'll just let Tigger out and grab a sweater," she said, letting them into her place.

Inside, Molly took Tigger out to the small, fenced yard behind her little place. When she came back in, Sam was sitting on the couch waiting. Tigger ran to him, leaping right onto his lap.

Sam's laughter made Molly smile. "Hey there. You just never stop being happy, do you?"

Katherine popped back into Molly's head. "Your mom got a little sad there."

Sam's eyes met hers and that sadness was reflected in his gaze, making Molly's heart contract painfully. She walked over and curled into his side, petting Tigger's head.

"Yeah. I saw that, too. Made me feel like a jerk for giving her a hard time about the sheriff. I want her to be happy."

"You're not a jerk. Not even close. It's normal for it to feel weird for you, I think. For her, too, I'd imagine."

They sat petting the dog, their fingers grazing. Molly rested her head on Sam's shoulder, enjoying the quiet and just being with him. She'd been reluctant to move their relationship along too quickly, thinking that was her downfall. Instead, they'd been moving very slowly, getting to know each other and spending time together. Was she holding back out of fear? Sam wouldn't hurt her the way her ex had. Or the ones before him.

Until Sam, she'd let herself jump in feet first, believing the best in people who hadn't earned that kind of faith. But Sam. Sam deserved her faith and her heart. He wouldn't step out on her, resent her career, push her away, or play games. *Maybe they were all just practice for the real thing so you'd recognize it when it showed up.*

"You still want to go?" Sam pressed a kiss to her forehead.

She leaned into him, inhaling deeply. He was the kind of man who would take care of her heart when she forgot to. "I do. You?"

He smiled at her, setting Tigger on the floor. "Absolutely. It's fun and there's ice cream."

She poked him in the belly. "You're hungry already?"

He leaned in, tunneling one hand into her hair at the back of her head and kissed her softly. She let herself fall into the feel of his lips against hers, the heat of his body pressing in close. When he leaned back, she let out a quick breath.

"It's really good ice cream," he answered, reminding her she'd asked a question.

"Let's go."

Sam stared at her another beat before standing up and taking her hand. The heat of his palm made her think something icy cold was exactly what she needed.

Chapter Five

Molly loved the time between the sun dipping into the sky and the star scattered darkness. There was something peaceful about that transition and living in Britton Bay, so close to the water, with not one skyscraper blocking the view, made it more magical. Sam's fingers linked with hers, a steady, but sweet reminder of her growing attachment to this place. These people. This man. She breathed through the thought and realized she got a little less scared every day. Perhaps she was more gun-shy of finding forever than she'd ever imagined. Not just with Sam, but with her home and finding a place to settle. Moving around, as a child, it had been hard to find a sense of permanency. It was only now that she suspected she'd stopped allowing herself to yearn for such a thing.

The laughter of kids floated into the air like the three balloons that randomly drifted by. Sam looked up and pointed.

"Uh-oh. Escapees."

"Hopefully there isn't a crying child somewhere," Molly said, watching them move across the water.

There were two long rows of vendors, one on each side of the sidewalk. When she'd heard about the end of summer celebration, she hadn't imagined it would be so…huge. *This town just keeps surprising you.* The scent of apple pie wafted through the air and Molly nearly sighed in pleasure. Nothing went better with ice cream than apple pie.

"You look so content," Sam noted, squeezing her hand.

She looked up at him as they strolled past a table with two women selling beaded bracelets and necklaces. "I have every reason to be." She stared at him a beat longer than usual so he understood that she realized he was a big part of that.

Leaning in for a quick kiss, he grinned. "Shop or sweets first?"

Molly bit her lip, but only hesitated a moment. "Let's browse until we find the first treat we want."

They stopped to look at some signs with vintage cars and cool phrases on them. Sam picked up a thin, rectangular one. It had the front end of a classic Corvair punched out to give a 3-D effect. Over the car, it read: WHAT HAPPENS IN THE GARAGE, then under the car, STAYS IN THE GARAGE.

"That's cute. You should get it," Molly said, eyeing the business cards. The sign behind the table said they did custom signs. Sam's birthday wasn't until closer to Christmas, but it might make a fun gift.

Sam side-eyed her with a wry grin. "Sure fire way to make any guy not buy anything? Tell him it's cute."

Molly swallowed a laugh and then made a second attempt. "Right. That is one tough looking sign. You should get it."

The guy watching them laughed. "Make you a deal, two for twenty."

Sam put it down. "Still just looking, but thanks."

Before they walked on, Molly grabbed a card and just grinned when Sam arched one of his brows at her as she pocketed it.

He waited patiently while she looked at wood painted signs. They had quotes and expressions on them and she was running her hand over one when he nudged her.

"You could make one of those," he whispered.

Molly glanced up to see the woman selling them was busy chatting with the person at the table next to her.

Still, she bumped his hip with hers. "Shh. That's not what they want to hear."

"Uh-oh. I think the new girl might still be more tourist than local," he teased.

Rolling her eyes, she took his hand. They weren't a quarter of the way down the first row before they ran into someone they knew.

Alan, her boss, was walking hand in hand with his wife. Knowing Vicky suffered from some health issues not long ago, Molly was very happy to see her out and looking so full of life.

"Molly!" Probably around the same age as Sam's mom, Vicky Benedict was a kind, soft-hearted woman. Molly had only met her a couple of times, but she embraced her like an old friend.

"It's good to see you." Molly pulled back and smiled at Alan.

Alan held out a hand that Sam accepted as they exchanged hellos. Vicky pressed a kiss to Sam's cheek.

"Look at you two together," Vicky said, clasping her hands together in front of her.

Sam laughed, but Molly felt the blush creep up her cheeks. He put a hand on the back of her neck and squeezed affectionately.

"Vicky," Alan said, amusement warming his tone.

She swatted at her husband. "What? I can't be happy for them?" She looked at them. "Sorry, can't help it. How's your mom, Sam?"

"She's good. Thanks for asking."

"You tell her I said hi. I need to visit with her one of these days," she said, stepping closer to Alan.

Alan put an arm around her and Molly's heart pulsed. His adoration of his wife was written all over his face. She knew, because they'd opened up to her a while back about Vicky's struggle with some social anxiety, among other things. Seeing her out and about like this was a good sign.

"She would really love that," Sam said.

"She's got her hands full right now," Alan said, a knowing smile on his lips.

"That she does," Molly agreed. "Speaking of which, I have an interview set up with Skyler Friessen tomorrow morning."

Alan's eyes widened. "That's a surprise. She didn't seem like the chatty type to me."

Molly still couldn't believe how abrupt she'd been on several occasions now. "Me neither. It'll make for an interesting side story to the wedding."

"Absolutely," Alan said. He gave a nod to someone passing by, then glanced at Vicky. "We should let them get back to their browsing."

"It was good to see you both. Together," Vicky said, making them laugh.

They said goodbye and carried on hand in hand. Molly stared after them for a moment. They wove their way through small pockets of people milling about, shopping, and chatting. Down on the beach, a huge game of Frisbee had started.

Molly pointed. "Tigger would love that."

Chuckling, Sam nodded. "He'd go crazy."

It was interesting, Molly decided, this blend of familiar and different. There were many vendors she recognized and several she didn't. A few of the extended stay tourists had been there almost as long as Molly. She knew some people had summer homes along the ocean. She'd seen several gorgeous ones when she'd gone to dinner one night at Alan and Vicky's.

Many of the tables carried similar things; wooden signage, handmade necklaces, and crochet dishcloths were popular items. Food tables were dispersed between trinkets and smelly soaps, breaking up the browsing with the chance to sample.

"Keep stealing bites of everything and you won't have room for ice cream," Sam teased her when she took a brownie bite from a plate that said, "Try me".

Popping the brownie in her mouth, she smiled around it. "You underestimate me."

A few tables down, she was grateful she hadn't stolen Sam's brownie bite as well. The Morning Muffins table had a well-deserved crowd. A couple of kids, a little girl in a bright pink sundress and a little boy with cropped blond hair, ran between them and the crowd, the girl giggling as the little boy reached for her. It made Molly smile, the simple sweetness of it. When they reached the table, there were several samples displayed, every one of them looking more delicious than the next. Behind the canopy that covered the table, a van was parked with a sign on the door that read MORNING MUFFINS. The back doors were open and Molly expected to greet Bella when someone closed one of the doors with a hip check. Instead, it was one of her employees, Georgina, who went by Georgie. She wasn't much older than Hannah and Molly had only met her once. Usually, she was shadowing Bella in the kitchen more than serving customers out front.

"Hey Sam," Georgie greeted, then looked at Molly with a smile just a little less radiant. "And Molly, right?"

Molly bit back her grin. She'd been told by Calli that while most people were happy Molly was settling in, a few women were disappointed that one of the quote unquote hot and good ones had been taken. "It is. Georgie, right?"

"Yup." She set down the white plastic bins she was carrying and grabbed a set of tongs.

"How's things, Georgie?" Sam picked up a piece of what looked like cinnamon scone and popped it in his mouth. Molly went for the double chocolate one and had no regrets. It melted on her tongue.

"Good. Summer is almost done, which means my hours will get cut back. I'm thinking of taking some classes at Oregon State."

"Hmm," Sam said, picking up another sample. "Jill went there for a semester I think. You should ask her about it."

The smile Georgie gave Sam was worthy of emeralds and diamonds. Molly nearly rolled her eyes at Sam's blindness toward the blatant adoration.

"That'd be great. I'll do that. I like working with Bella, but even she said, if I ever wanna strike out on my own, I need business classes."

A woman reached around Molly to grab the last bite of chocolate scone, but thankfully, that was the bin Georgie just opened. Using the tongs, she set more onto the empty plate.

"I'm surprised Bella isn't here tonight," Molly said, trying to decide between the chocolate scone and some sort of delicate berry filled pastry.

Georgie made a strange noise, almost a cross between a huff and a snort. "Me, too. But she was too wound up. Said she was working her grumpies out on the dough." Then Georgie laughed and shook her head, looking right at Sam. "She's like a Disney cartoon or something. Even when she's mad, she's cute and sweet. I mean, who says 'grumpies'?"

Molly and Sam both laughed, but Molly couldn't help wondering what Bella was grumpy about. She wondered if things were okay between the baker and Callan. Georgie moved down the table for a moment, helping a little girl reach a cookie sample.

"Don't think I've ever seen Bella in a bad mood," Sam said, then winced. He, of course, knew that Molly hadn't been the baker's favorite person for a short period of time. "Sorry."

"It's okay. I feel like things are smoothing over. Though, if I'm honest, I still wonder about her and Callan."

Sam stroked a hand down her hair then pressed a kiss to her head. "I know, honey. But he's a good guy. Not as good as your guy, but that's asking a lot."

Molly laughed, leaning into him. When Georgie wandered back over, Molly chose a box of muffins to take home. While she dug money out of her purse, it was Sam who voiced her question.

"What was Bella wound up about?"

Georgie took the money from Molly and dug in her apron for change. "She went over to meet the chef. You know the one who is catering the wedding? Thought it would be nice to offer the use of her ovens if the ones at your mom's place aren't enough."

Molly accepted her change. "I'm guessing Skyler wasn't receptive?"

"You know her?" Georgie frowned.

"I've been introduced to her, but no, not really." Molly didn't tell the young woman that just meeting Skyler for a few minutes would be enough to wind most people up. She wasn't exactly receptive and Molly could just imagine how curtly she'd refused Bella's offer.

"My mom feels bad that she canceled her regular orders for the next few days," Sam said.

The small-town camaraderie was one of the things Molly loved about Britton Bay. The businesses supported each other, just like the people.

Katherine kept Bella's goods on hand while the baker kept a rack of pamphlets featuring the bed-and-breakfast in her shop.

Georgie waved her hand. "Aw. Bella knows your mom didn't have much say in it. She's not upset about that. And she'll be over this before the night is out, I'm sure."

"Hope so. Tell her everything is delicious as always," Molly said as Sam slipped his hand against hers.

"I will."

"Excuse me, Georgie, do you have any bumbleberry pie left?" A woman Molly had seen a few times in the bakery nudged her way to the front of the table, angling herself so she cut Molly and Sam off. Her dark red hair was a mass of wide curls that framed her face. Sam grinned.

"Hey Mrs. Harver," he said.

She looked at him, her aging eyes squinting to see who was saying hello. There were more wrinkles on her face than lines on a map and she got a kick out of telling anyone who'd listen that she'd earned every one of them.

"Hello, Sam. How are you doing?"

"Good ma'am. You?"

She preened a little, running a hand down the front of her blue zip up hoodie that matched her blue jogging pants. Molly bit her lip.

"I'm very well. And you? We haven't met yet. Is Sam courting you?"

Molly swallowed her giggle. "I believe he's trying to, yes. I'm Molly Owens. It's a pleasure to meet you Mrs. Harver."

They shook hands and Molly just knew she was being sized up. She had stolen the town's most eligible bachelor according to the high school newspaper, which was run by Hannah.

"And you. I've heard good things about you and I like what you're doing with the paper. For a while, the only time I read it was when I needed a good sedative. It's a lot more upbeat now and I sure do like the 'Say Anything' feature. I'll be writing into that one for sure."

Sam squeezed her hand and they chatted for another moment before continuing on their walk.

"Did you see the 'Say Anything' section?" Molly asked as they strolled past more of the vendors with only a cursory glance. The sky was getting darker and the first hint of stars were peeking out through the night.

Sam, who'd grabbed a sample of cookie before leaving the table, finished chewing before answering. "I did. Thought it was pretty funny. Risky though, letting people share their open opinions."

Wrapping her arm around his biceps, she leaned closer. "Don't worry. the *Britton Bay Bulletin* has an excellent editor that vets each submission and makes necessary adjustments."

"I figured. Should be fun to see what people say. Mrs. Harver tells everyone she used to be a Hollywood starlet. She's probably got some stories to share," he said.

"Wouldn't that be fun?"

They stopped near a flagstone path that led from the sidewalk to the sand. Together, they stared at the water, taking a moment of quiet and enjoying the gentle lap of the waves.

By the time they browsed a few more tables and got their ice cream, the stars were out in full force. Walking back to the bed-and-breakfast, Molly yawned. The closer they got, the more she imagined how nice it would be if he didn't just kiss her goodbye at the door like most nights. How nice it would be to have him come in, curl up on the couch and when both of them were ready to call it a day, curl into her bed together. She missed living with someone, but the last experience had left her more than a little jaded. The next time she shared a home with someone, she'd be a lot more certain of the person's character. She had no doubt about Sam's, but she didn't want to rush. She liked this feeling—him courting her. She smiled at the thought. She started to tell him how cute she thought it was that Mrs. Harver had asked, but an angry voice stopped her.

Sam pulled her to a stop just as they reached the magnolia tree at the side of his mother's home. They were about to step onto the path that led around the back or the front and would take her to her own cottage.

"What do you want?" a male voice hissed.

Molly looked at Sam. "Should we go around?" She whispered so low she wondered if he heard.

"I wanted to see if it was actually you," a female voice replied. They weren't overly loud and clearly they were on the side of the house away from the wedding setup. They weren't exactly quiet either.

Sam put a finger to his lips and pulled Molly closer so they huddled behind the tree. Like her, he probably thought it was too awkward to try and go around either way. So they stayed still, breathing in each other's air while they unintentionally eavesdropped. Molly couldn't see anything through the trees and even though the moon shone bright, it didn't cast its glow through the branches and shaded area of the side of the house.

"It's me. Now you know. Now let's pretend it never happened." The man sounded angry.

"Aw, why? Would that upset her?" Disdain and false injury rang out from the female voice that Molly struggled to recognize. It was familiar.

"You can't say a thing. I'm warning you. I'm *begging* you," the man's voice said.

"Not the first time you've done that," came the female reply.

"Don't. It was a mistake. Don't make it something it wasn't. You're in a good place, I'm in a good place. Please, please let it go."

"Or what?"

Sam and Molly locked eyes.

"Or you'll regret it."

Shuffling movement had them both easing back because it sounded close. She realized one of them had stalked off when she heard footsteps on the concrete stairs at the side of the house. If someone was heading that way, around the back of the house, which way would the other person go? When they heard nothing else after a few minutes, Sam took a step forward, around the tree and looked down the path.

"They're gone," he whispered. "One of them must have gone around the front."

Molly nodded. "The other went around the back, so it's most likely a guest."

Sam's hand came to her back and he, too, looked around the darkened yard. It was pointless, as there was nothing to see.

"Wonder what that was," Sam said, his voice still low.

Molly looked up at him, no longer sleepy. "I don't know *what*, but I know *who* one of them was."

"Which one?"

"The woman. That was Skyler Friessen's voice."

Chapter Six

Molly woke just before seven and took Tigger on a quicker than usual stroll. When she'd first arrived, she'd explored different hikes and routes before she found one she loved. It took them down to the ocean via some steps and if she walked along the shore, she'd come up near Main Street. This morning she'd turn back once they made it to the water. There was no way she'd be late for her interview with Skyler. *How can I possibly work in a question about last night? It's none of your business.* Somehow, that didn't make it less interesting. Who would she fight with? *There was the male sous chef.*

Tigger tugged, pulling her out of her thoughts. It was a surprise to see the beach so quiet. Other than a couple strolling, hand in hand way down the sand, they had the area to themselves. Molly was looking forward to experiencing Britton Bay in the quiet season. When she'd arrived, the season was just picking up and there was plenty going on. It would be interesting to see what sort of articles and stories they'd deliver to the town when there wasn't much happening.

"We might have the beach all to ourselves all the time now," she said to Tigger as they rounded a crop of rocks that teenagers had drawn and written all over. New hashtags got added frequently. Today, the most vibrant ones read: #givelove #gotlove. A lot nicer than any of the graffiti she'd seen in California.

Molly sat on one of the logs and let Tigger romp around since there was no one to bother. The tide was out and lapping waves were like therapy for her busy mind. She could almost shut off the constant questions and wondering that took up too much space in her brain when she zoned in on the water.

Tigger bounded up to the white crests and then ran away like they'd spooked him. Molly laughed and the sound carried away on the breeze. Gulls flew overhead and Molly looked up, gazing at the early morning sky. It was beautiful here. Her parents were thinking of coming for a visit in the next couple of months. She'd wanted time to settle first. *And to decide if you were going to stay.*

She thought of the way Sam kissed her, of how she knew people when she took Tigger out, how Katherine was a perfect blend between motherly and friendly.

"Definitely staying."

Whistling for Tigger, she waited until he joined her then reattached his leash. "Time to go, bud."

As they started walking back to the stairs that would lead up to the road and take her home, a flash of yellow caught her eye. Molly walked up to a massive, hollowed out tree trunk. Tigger's tail went crazy and he pulled at the leash. The sand scrunched under her running shoes as she kept up his pace. When she rounded the tree, she saw Chantel sitting, back against it. Her blonde hair was in a high ponytail and she wore a pair of dark leggings with an oversized sweater. Her perfect, alabaster skin was blotchy and tears still marked her cheeks. She sniffed loudly.

"Chantel?"

She startled and turned her head to look at Molly. Tigger stretched forward, doing his best to crawl onto her. To Molly's surprise, the woman reached out as she leaned forward and pet his head.

"Do I know you?"

Stepping closer so Tigger didn't hurt himself, Molly shook her head. "No. I live in the cottage at the bed-and-breakfast. I recognized you as the bride-to-be. Are you...okay?"

Chantel sniffled again and pulled a Kleenex out of her pocket, wiping her nose. The polished, seemingly high maintenance woman Molly had seen was gone. This woman seemed normal, approachable, and incredibly sad.

"I'm fine. Just emotional I guess. That cottage is cute. I'd originally asked if my fiancé and I could stay there. Katherine said it was rented out. I wanted a bit of space from the bridal party. And my mom."

Molly couldn't fault the woman for that. "I can imagine with only a few days left to go, you've got a lot on your plate. Everything at the house looks beautiful though. And from what I could smell last night when I popped into the kitchen, the food is going to be amazing."

Continuing to pet Tigger, who'd flopped down in the sand, Chantel looked away. "Yes. It'll be amazing no matter what the cost. My mother would have it no other way."

Shaking her head like she'd just snapped out of a trance, Chantel stood and dusted herself off. "I need to get back. The bridesmaids she enlisted insisted on a spa day."

Scrunching her brows, she asked hesitantly, "Enlisted?"

The smile Chantel gave her was forced. "Of course. You can't have just anyone stand up for you at your wedding. What would people think?" She rolled her eyes. "Oh, well. I can't believe this town even has a spa. It seems so tiny and the way my mom always talked about her hometown, I was expecting to feel like a pioneer in the olden days.

Molly bit her tongue so she didn't scoff. They were a smaller town for sure, but Portland was only a couple of hours away. They weren't exactly in the middle of nowhere. Tugging at Tigger's leash so Chantel could step around her, Molly noted she looked more composed. She'd effectively put her mask back in place.

"See you around."

Molly didn't bother to remind her they were heading to the same place. She didn't exactly exude a welcoming-walk-back-with-me vibe.

She and Tigger waited a few moments then started up the steps. Tummy growling, Molly wondered if she had time to stop by Bella's for some scones.

"Maybe I'll just grab some cereal this morning." It would be safer and quicker. Then she remembered she'd grabbed some muffins the night before and her mood improved.

* * * *

Molly didn't see anyone when she returned home. It still seemed strange to her that the wedding party, bride and groom and all, had come so early. In California, she'd had a couple of invites for bachelorette parties that involved weekends in Vegas. What happened to just a fun night of laughing and dancing with friends to celebrate your upcoming marriage?

"Like you know anything about marriage or commitment. You're freaking out because you want Sam to stay the night."

Tigger looked at her and she realized she'd spoken out loud. Technically, Sam had stayed the night, but only to comfort her after the woman who'd killed Vernon East had tried to do away with Molly as well. Molly shivered and got into her Jeep, nerves and excitement pumping to the same beat.

Now and again, she still had vivid dreams of finding Vernon dead, but she tried not to think about it or push away the thoughts when they came. Sam had stayed with her that night and held her safe in his arms through until morning. She'd slept better than she had in a really long time.

Pulling out of the driveway, she passed a large flower delivery van. Looks like the guests would be waking up any minute to start the day of festivities. Molly turned on Brewster, the road before Main Street. The only hotel in Britton Bay was about a five-minute walk from all of the shops and the beach. There was also a motel and a few other bed-and-breakfasts, but none like Katherine's.

Seaside Shangri-La was a four-story rectangular building. The top floor offered views of the ocean and Jacuzzi tubs. Molly had considered staying there her first few days in town, but had opted for the motel instead because it had a diner attached. Though, once she'd checked out the food on Main Street, she hadn't gone back.

The outside of the building was plain, beige stucco, but each room boasted a wide balcony. There was a swimming pool on the grounds, as well as a half dozen cottage units that sat poolside. Molly turned left toward the parking lot, which was across from the cabins. Surprise had her pumping the brakes. What were the police doing at the hotel? A couple of cruisers sat parked at an angle toward one of the units. They'd obviously arrived in a hurry.

"Probably a drunk and disorderly," she said aloud, pulling into the lot. "Or Corky causing a fuss."

Corky Templeton was the so-called "town crazy." According to Calliope—who owned the Come 'n Get It Eatery, Corky had been hit by lightning several times and the town looked at him as a sort of mascot. They all took turns feeding him, giving him clothing or shelter when he needed it and, if he was having a bad day, helping him calm down. No one appeared to know the true story of what made Corky the way he was, but there was a softness in the man's eyes that made Molly sad. She couldn't help but wonder how in a town full of history, no one knew his.

Glancing back and forth between the hotel and the people milling about the cabins, Molly wondered if Skyler had told the front desk that she was expecting a visitor this early. Or at all. Getting out of the Jeep, purse slung over her shoulder, Molly saw Corky peeking around the front corner of the hotel, watching the police activity. She made her way over to him cautiously so she wouldn't startle him.

Corky was wringing his hands together. He wore fingerless gloves and an oversized coat—despite the heat—that he had zipped up to his bushy-haired chin. When he turned and saw Molly, he clapped his gloved hands together.

"She's not all right. Just brushing her teeth then she fell. I didn't touch her. I didn't. I saw the stars. The stars are dark." He was moving his hands quicker now and looking around the corner, pacing between the building and Molly.

Unsure how to ease his obviously distraught state, she stepped in from of him so he had to stop in his tracks. "Hi Corky. Everything okay?" She'd yet to have a completely understandable conversation with him since she'd moved to town, but never had he seemed so agitated in her presence.

He froze in front of her and stared at her like *she* was the one spouting nonsense. "No more stars. I wanted to go swimming. I came to go swimming. I was going to go swimming and she fell."

Molly tried to smile, but her confusion made it difficult. Who was he talking about? She glanced back at the police cars. Had there been an accident? She focused on the last part of what he'd said. The only part she could help with. "You can swim in the ocean, Corky."

He shook his head. "It's not safe. Nowhere is safe."

"It's safe. You can swim at main beach," she said, wondering if he was disoriented about where he was. "Do you want me to take you there?"

Corky pointed at the pool. "I just wanted to swim. Sometimes I swim. I don't get in trouble for swimming if no one is watching."

Perhaps he'd been caught and gotten in trouble? He started wringing his hands again, like he couldn't warm them despite the gloves. The smell of his breath and unwashed clothes reminded her that if he hadn't showered, the management would be quite upset—rightly so—about him swimming in their guest pool. That might not be the reason for the police, but it could definitely explain the homeless man's near hysteria.

"Can I do anything for you, Corky?"

He shook his head again, staring at her like a lost soul. "No. Nothing can be done."

She hesitated, not wanting to leave him like this, but in truth, he was always somewhat like this. Molly patted his arm and made her way down the sidewalk and into the hotel, making a mental note to bring him a coffee and muffin the next time he was around the *Britton Bay Bulletin*.

The lobby was well lit and had bonus lighting coming from the wall of automatic sliding doors. The bellman also functioned as the concierge, front desk clerk and, if necessary, a maid.

Molly had seen him in the diner and since Calliope's goal was for Molly to have the scoop on absolutely everyone in town, she knew his name was

Kip Martin. His dark face was a study in tension, his lips drawn down, his eyes darting up and down, then locking on hers.

"Good morning. Molly, right? I don't think we've met."

He extended his hand as Molly approached the counter and she shook it. "No, we haven't. You're Kip right? It's nice to meet you."

"You as well, though I hope you're not checking in, as we are, um… experiencing an issue."

An issue? What did that mean? She put her arms on the counter, folding them over one another. "Actually, I'm here to interview one of your guests. Skyler Friessen."

She tried not to ask, but couldn't help herself. She leaned forward, not noticing the way his hands gripped the edge of the counter. "What's with the cops out back? Everything okay? I saw Corky and he was pretty flustered."

"You can't interview Skyler." Kip's voice came out like gravel pouring down a rickety slide.

"She's expecting me."

He shook his head. "You don't understand."

Surely the cook hadn't changed her mind and left a message with the front desk to tell Molly she was unavailable.

"Maybe you could call her and tell her I'm here. I promised I wouldn't take much of her time."

Kip leaned forward, looking left and right despite the empty lobby. "She can't be interviewed. She's dead."

Chapter Seven

Molly stared at the front desk clerk, unsure she'd really heard what she'd heard. Dead? How? Why? Her heart skipped a few beats like it needed to lay down for a rest. Then it was up and off like a shot, pounding so hard in her chest, her breath caught.

"I'm sorry. Did you say dead?" She whispered the words as she leaned across the counter.

Creases formed around his eyes as he squeezed them shut and nodded in slow motion. When he opened them, his gaze shouted with misery.

"Good thing it's the end of the summer or this would seriously impact business."

Molly's eyes widened. "A guest died and you're worried about business?" She pulled her phone out of her purse, irritation bubbling.

He had the decency to look down and mutter an apology. "As far as guests go, she wasn't exactly nice." His tone was defensive.

Molly texted Alan and Elizabeth to let them know the little she knew. *You chastised him for thinking about business while you're thinking in headlines.* Still, people had to know and it was better to get accurate information out to the public rather than frenzied gossip.

"That's why the police are here?"

Kip nodded. "They've been here for over an hour. They've got the catering crew. What do you call it when they can't leave?"

"Sequestered?"

He pointed at her. "Yes. And the staff from last night have to come in. Everyone has to be questioned."

Were they being questioned as witnesses to events or as suspects? She wondered if they already had a suspect in mind and Molly's thoughts jumped back to the argument from the night before. "Did she have any visitors?"

"None that checked in, but the cabins are kind of an anomaly now since the fence that enclosed them was taken down to be replaced."

Molly frowned. "There hasn't been a fence since I moved here." The area was wide open, but the pool was still enclosed.

"Exactly. It's never been put back up so it limits our security."

A woman came through a door behind the counter. Her curly red hair made her look like Raggedy Ann. "Kip, the police want surveillance footage. I'll watch the front."

Kip sighed. "Okay." Then he looked at Molly. "You helped find Vernon's killer when he was killed, right?"

She nodded, unsure where he was going with this. Her phone buzzed in her hand with a useless update. Nothing like death to make all other things seem inconsequential in comparison.

"Can they blame me if I'm in charge of the hotel? Like negligence or something, like when a person gets drunk and is in an accident and the bartender can be blamed?"

Arching a brow at his train of thought, she shook her head slowly. "I don't believe you can be responsible for her death just by renting her a room. Unless you are connected directly to her death."

Another thought struck her at that moment: *Skyler was a miserable woman—unfriendly as well as unhappy. Did she end her own life?*

She wanted to ask, but couldn't form the words. Instead, before Kip slipped out the door, she asked, "Who found her?"

Kip turned. "Corky Templeton."

Molly groaned. No wonder he'd been even more off than usual. She left through the front of the hotel, going back to where she'd seen the homeless man but he wasn't there. Walking around the hotel, she saw the coroner had arrived. Other patrons were gathered around the police tape and barricades that had been set up. She spotted Officer Chris Beatty, Sam's friend, speaking to a couple of people as he urged them to step further back. He saw her approach and she was almost positive she saw his jaw tighten.

Chris had been kind to her during the investigation into Vernon's death and she and Sam had hung out with him and his girlfriend Sarah more than once. Right now, however, he was in full-on cop mode. A shadow of dark stubble covered his chin and his dark hair was tousled, like he'd been awoken before he was ready.

"Molly." His tone lacked inflection, a clear sign that he was in all-business mode.

She slipped on her own professional persona, despite the fact that her mind felt like it was riding an out of control Ferris wheel. "Officer Beatty. It's my understanding that Corky Templeton found celebrity chef, Skyler Friessen, dead in her hotel room?"

Moving one of the ropes that was assisting with keeping people out, Officer Beatty came closer. Over his shoulder, she saw a stretcher being brought into cabin number four.

"Molly, this is an ongoing investigation. You know I can't tell you anything."

For a second, she wanted to apologize and walk away. *You're standing on front page news and would expect anyone, including Hannah, to get details for a story the* Britton Bay Bulletin *is obligated to write.*

"I know you can't say much, but you know as well as I do, gossip will spread through town before the sun is even all the way in the sky. Was she murdered?"

The tense set of his lips belayed his frustration. "We're still assessing the situation. At the moment, we cannot release any details to members of the press."

Ouch. She arched a brow. "I guess I'll gather information from the gossip that comes in this afternoon. Thanks for your time."

She turned and nearly smiled when she felt his hand on her arm. Turning back, she tried for a neutral expression.

He leaned in. "We're still looking into possible foul play. The victim was found on the floor near the door, which was ajar. An early morning swimmer said he saw Corky walking toward it, pushing it open, and screaming. The woman died brushing her teeth from what we can see. That's it. I've sent some officers out to canvas and we're dealing with it one step at a time. Don't print anything yet, but that's what we have so far. If you can keep details out of the paper for now, I'll share what I can as soon as I can."

Molly smiled, but it felt bittersweet. "Thanks Chris. Awful way for you to start your day."

He looked back at the cottages then down at Molly. "Hers was worse."

She watched him walk away and noticed Corky hadn't left the area. He hovered near the corner of the far cottage, watching, like he was scared, but couldn't stop looking. She died brushing her teeth. That's what Corky had said. Had she been getting ready for bed and gotten a knock at the door? Molly had done that: carried on getting ready for her day while grabbing a newspaper from the front stoop. *Everyday normal activities. No big deal. We worry about accidents and disasters and really, you could die right in the middle of your regular routine.* The thought terrified Molly so she pushed it out of her head.

* * * *

Unsure whether she should head home and see if Katherine needed anything or if she should go into work, Molly sat in her Jeep trying to process it all. She watched as police officers and curious bystanders moved around the scene. She'd been face to face with a crime scene when she'd discovered Vernon dead on his living room floor. The memory sent a shiver through her body. She could go her whole life without ever seeing something like that again.

When her phone buzzed, she jumped. It was Sam so she slid her thumb across the screen.

"Hey."

"Hey," he said. "You okay?" His voice was warm, wrapping around her like a hug.

"I don't know."

"You heard about the chef?" he asked.

She tightened her fingers on the phone, watching as people made way for crime scene techs. Did crime scene techs come to suicides? *No one said suicide. But who would kill her—she didn't even know anyone here. Maybe someone she came with?*

"I did. How did *you*?"

"My mom. According to her, Patty was trying to contact the chef this morning for some menu changes and when she couldn't get through, she called the front desk, flipped out on the guy when he said he couldn't connect her and then the guy told her she was dead. Patty went to my mom, freaking out about the wedding being ruined."

Molly closed her eyes. Never mind the fact that someone had lost their life—the woman was worried about the wedding. "It's barely eight o'clock. How can so much happen before noon in this town?"

His laugh didn't ring with the usual joviality, but still, it settled her stomach. "Not the sleepy-nothing-ever-happens-place California was, is it?"

A smile tugged at her lips, despite the situation. "No. Not at all. I'm trying to decide if I should head home and see if your mom needs anything or if I should go to work. I don't see Patty or her daughter making the day easy on your mom."

"I've got Critter covering my jobs today, so I'm heading over to see if I can do anything."

She shook her head, scrunching up her face. "Why do you guys call him that?" She'd only met the mechanic once and he seemed perfectly nice for such a weird nickname.

"You don't want to know."

She sighed. "Probably not. Okay, I'll head to the paper, but will you text me if Katherine needs anything?"

"How about I text you even if she doesn't?"

This time her lips just turned up without warning. "That sounds good. Sam…"

"Hmm?"

What? What did she want to say? It felt like words were spinning around in her heart and her chest, but they were all crashing into each other like bumper cars, leaving her with nothing.

"I'll see you later."

"Sounds good."

They hung up and she waited a few more minutes while the coroner's vehicle drove off. Police officers continued to chat with people and the door to Skyler's room was still open. She didn't see Corky anywhere now. Maybe one of the officers had taken him into custody. Now and again, they'd bring him into the station, get him warmed up and fed. Had he seen anything significant? She hated seeing him so flustered. *Maybe I should just head to the paper.* She stared out the window, watching people watch. It made her feel like she was removed from the situation. Like she was watching the making of one of those cop shows. *If the cops and coroner were already there, what time did they find her?* Molly shivered, thinking about the argument from the night before. She and Sam had gone back to the house around ten.

Molly squeezed the steering wheel tight. Her phone buzzed, breaking through the strange trance she felt locked in. Surprise scrunched her eyebrows together when she saw it was Bella calling. As she answered, she saw some of the catering staff, including the male sous chef, huddled in one of the other cabin doorways. Perhaps sequestered was too strong a term if they could watch what was happening.

"Hi Bella," she greeted.

"Molly. Can you come to the bakery?"

The male chef lit a cigarette and moved out of the huddle, swiped at his left eye with the sleeve of his shirt.

"Uh, I'm actually heading into work. Can I stop by later today?" She'd told Chris gossip would fly, but she didn't want to be the one to set it free. Still, she had to bite down on her tongue so she didn't explain her current whereabouts. She wondered how people who'd been on the receiving end of Skyler's sharp tongue would feel about her death. *If it's murder, someone might be feeling guilty. Or vindicated.*

Bella sniffled loudly into the receiver, redirecting all of Molly's attention.

"Please, Molly. I need your help. A police officer was just here."

"What? Why?" Molly started her Jeep.

"She wanted to question me about Skyler Friessen's death."

Air trapped itself in Molly's lungs, making her chest ache from the pressure. "I'll be there in ten minutes."

She hung up and pulled out of the lot. Traffic was rarely a problem in Britton Bay and this morning was no different. The hotel was snuggled in between clusters of trees with beach access. There were more people standing around the cabins than at the beach, but she was sure that would change as the day progressed. She still couldn't believe that there'd been another death. She shivered at the thought, her skin feeling itchy and tight.

Despite being an editor, death was something she read about online or in the news. She'd never had it so close to home and now, within the span of three months, she knew two people who'd died. Vernon's death had been a shock—actually seeing a lifeless body was something she'd never forget. Would Corky? On television, people rushed to the bodies and felt for a pulse or listened for breathing. When she'd stumbled upon Vernon, there'd been no need. Should she have done that? Rushed to the body to check for signs of life when there were clearly none? At least Corky had screamed. She didn't for a second believe that he had anything to do with Vernon's death. Corky was harmless. Sadly, he would now also be scarred with the memory of what he'd seen today.

She pulled up to the bakery in under the ten minutes she promised and was surprised to see a closed sign on the door. Getting out of her Jeep, she debated going to the back of the building, but like she'd been watching for her, Bella appeared through the glass and hurried to unlock the door. Mr. Elbury, who owned the pet store next door to Morning Muffins, pushed open his door just as Bella did hers.

"Morning Molly!" He gave a friendly wave then glanced at Bella. "You all right, dear? You're always open earlier than I am."

Bella looked at the store proprietor as if he'd spoken in a strange language. It was then Molly noticed the puffy redness around Bella's eyes. She started to speak and a tear trickled down her cheek.

Molly stepped forward, putting a hand on Bella's shoulder, and waving to Mr. Elbury said, "Bella's not feeling good this morning. One of those nasty summer colds. Have a good day, Mr. Elbury."

The older man frowned, running a hand over his gray beard. "Oh. Okay. Feel better. I'll bring you over some soup later. You know my Celia makes the best soup in town."

Bella still said nothing, but at least she nodded.

Molly widened her smile. "Don't let Calliope hear you say that."

He laughed, as she'd intended and then Molly nudged Bella so they went inside before he engaged them in a full conversation about his wife's soup making prowess.

When Bella's hands shook as she turned the lock, concern bolted through Molly's entire being. "Bella, what's wrong? What's going on?"

The baker, who at twenty-five ran one of the most successful shops on the strip, pulled in a shuddering breath. Her light brown hair was pulled back into a messy pony-tail, wisps of hair escaping the band. She shook her head and wrapped herself in a hug, her fingers digging into her own biceps. Just as Georgie had mentioned, it was rare to see Bella mad; it was also rare to see her so flustered.

"A police officer just stopped by and asked me about Skyler Friessen and whether or not I knew she was dead."

Molly put an arm around Bella and pulled her farther into the bakery. The right wall, which butted up against the pet store exterior, had no windows so Molly chose a table there and guided the shaking woman to a seat.

"Why on earth would they ask you if you knew?" One thing Molly had learned through years of editing people's thoughts and words was that what others said, was not always what the listener heard. People shifted words in their brains, attaching emotion and meaning to sometimes meaningless statements.

Bella sniffled again, fresh tears filling her eyes. "Because the last thing she drank was one of my lattes."

Chapter Eight

Molly knew the baker was out of sorts when she said nothing about Molly slipping behind the counter to make some tea. The display case was full of fresh pastries, muffins, and cinnamon buns. Molly's stomach growled but she ignored it and set about making two cups of regular tea. Bella sat at the table, looking down at her folded hands, sniffling quietly. Opening one of the small fridges under the counter, Molly grabbed some milk and added it to both cups. When she put it away, she noticed that the cash register had a balance.

"Were you already open this morning?" Molly asked, bringing the steaming mugs over. If nothing else, the tea would soothe the chill of this morning's events.

Bella nodded, accepting the tea. "We opened at five like usual. Actually, Trina opened this morning. I came down at seven and by seven-thirty the officer showed up."

Molly frowned, blew on her tea, wrapping her hands around the mug. "Was it busy?"

In a town like Britton Bay, most of the customers were regulars but there was still a steady stream of strangers stopping by most of the local businesses. But at five a.m.? Anyone who wasn't a regular would have to stand out.

Bella shrugged. "Trina didn't say anything about it being any busier than usual."

Sighing, Molly set her mug down. "Bella, are you okay?"

The woman frowned at her, setting her tea down with a bang. Liquid sloshed over the sides and Bella teared up again as Molly grabbed napkins from the dispenser and sopped up the mess.

"Of course I'm not okay. I was questioned by the police." She wiped around her mug with a napkin then took the crumpled, wet wad and slipped out from the booth, taking it to the trash.

When she came back, her eyes were dry. She stopped at the table and looked down at Molly.

"I'm sorry. I'm being snappy."

"That'll happen when you're questioned about a death."

Bella slipped back into the booth. "The truth is, I was running behind this morning because Callan and I got in an argument. When I arrived, I was already frazzled and I felt horrible for leaving Trina on her own for the morning rush."

Molly's brain twisted and turned with questions. What had she and Callan fought about? *That's irrelevant.* Though, the last time she'd looked into a murder, she'd learned no detail was irrelevant. *You are not looking into a murder!*

"What did the police ask you?" Molly itched to take out a notebook. Not necessarily to make notes, but just to have something to do with her hands. She picked up her tea instead, sipping carefully.

"Did I know Skyler. Did she come in this morning, did I go to her, had we argued, did anyone from her staff come by, where was I between midnight and six o'clock this morning."

That sounds like a timeframe for her death. "That's a lot of questions. What did you say?"

Bella leaned back against the cushion of the booth. "I just told them the truth. I didn't know the chef, I hadn't seen her, why would I go visit her, I don't know her staff and at six o'clock I was arguing with my boyfriend who doesn't want me to call him boyfriend because apparently that's juvenile."

Molly cringed. She hadn't given Callan a fair shake when she'd met him, but knowing he'd make Bella feel bad didn't warm her over. What chilled her more, however, was knowing Bella was lying. Even if she didn't know about the beverage, Georgie had said Bella went there the night before. And had come back abnormally upset.

A buzzer rang and Bella bolted upright, as if surprised. "I forgot, I put a batch of scones in."

She hurried toward the kitchen and turned for only a second when Molly called her name.

"Where's the staff? Where's Trina?"

"I sent them home. I may not have a summer cold, but I'm definitely not feeling well today."

Molly sat at the table, trying to figure out if the reason for the officer's visit this morning was solely because of a latte with Bella's business symbol on it. Did Chris know that Bella had gone to see the chef about the ovens and left angry? Had someone pointed him in Bella's direction? And since when did lattes kill? She'd heard of death by chocolate, but death by coffee?

Her phone chimed in her purse so she dug it out and answered when she saw Alan's name.

"Hey."

"Hi. I'm just checking in to see if you're alright." His voice was tired.

She appreciated his concern. "I am. The police were there when I arrived but something came up and I'm meeting with Bella."

She hoped he didn't press for answers on that since she didn't have any.

Alan's deep sigh sounded through the receiver. "Didn't we just put a death behind us? I thought we'd be able to focus on the merriment of a wedding. On something happy. Who on earth would kill a chef with no ties to this town?"

Molly didn't know, but the lives of several people she cared for would be tipped upside down if they didn't find out reasonably soon.

Bella came back to the table carrying a plate of four, fresh apple cinnamon scones with a cream-cheese drizzle.

Molly's mouth watered. "I need to go. Alan, are you guys okay at the paper today? I'd like to go back to the bed-and-breakfast and see about talking to the wedding staff and perhaps the wedding party."

And the man who argued with Skyler last night.

"Of course. Keep me posted. I'll see you later.'

She hung up and smiled at Bella who seemed more composed. "These smell delicious. Did you bring anything for you to eat?" Molly pulled the plate toward her with a grin and as she hoped, Bella gave a small smile.

"I'm not hungry."

Molly selected one of the scones after grabbing a napkin. She broke it apart and inhaled the cinnamon-scented steam. The woman was a genius with flour. If Chantel's family had done their research, they could have saved themselves a lot of headache by hiring local. *No outside ingredients.* Katherine had said the chef had strict guidelines. Molly's thoughts popped back to Chantel crying earlier that morning and wondered at the timing. She forgot about everything, though, when she took her first bite and the scone all but melted on her tongue.

"Molly."

Looking at her…were they friends now? She decided to be positive. They were friends. Maybe Bella would confide in her.

"Yeah?"

"There's something I didn't tell the police."

Even having an inkling of what Bella was going to say, her stomach dropped, like the bite of scone had been weighted down with a rock. No longer hungry, herself, she pushed the plate forward and leaned on the table.

"What, Bella?"

Bella's lips pursed up, like she wasn't sure she should say it out loud.

"I did go to see Skyler last night," she whispered.

Her eyes fluttered shut and when she opened them, they were glassy. "Nothing happened," Bella said. "I stopped by to let her know if they needed anything such as off-site cooking facilities, they were welcome to use my ovens."

Molly shook her head. At least that matched Georgie's story, which was a relief. Bella just didn't suit the role of liar. And Molly had only known her for a few months. The police officer had probably lived in Britton Bay for far longer and must know that Bella was no more a murderer than liar. *It's routine. Or, they know something you don't. Which would make sense since you're not a cop and not supposed to be getting wrapped up in this.* But Bella had called her and she was determined to prove to her that she wanted the woman's friendship.

"Okay. That's really nice. But why didn't you tell them?"

"Because they'd come to ask me about her death and I panicked."

That was understandable. The idea of death shook everyone up, but to have it so close to home was more than unsettling. It was completely unnerving.

She reached across the table and covered Bella's cold hand with her own. "Bella. I'm sure that it'll be okay. You can tell Chris that. Officer Beatty? I'm sure he'll understand."

Bella looked down at the table and Molly's stomach flopped like a kid diving off the highest board.

"What else, Bella?"

"Trina didn't know why the police were here. They often come in for coffee, like everyone else. So when the officer came to the counter and asked if she knew about the celebrity chef in town, Trina said yes, but her name wasn't allowed to be said in the bakery."

Cringing, she patted Bella's hand and pulled hers back. She wondered if Georgie had gossiped about her boss's reaction or if Trina had been working the evening before as well. "That's okay. It was a joke, right?"

Eyes crinkled and mouth turned down, Bella nodded. "Sort of. When I got back last night, after talking to Skyler, I may have said something about her being an uppity wench who wouldn't know good food if it smacked her in the face. Then I might have said her name was a curse word in this place and my staff better watch their words. But I was just mad, Molly. She riled me up, she was so rude and dismissive. She told me she'd rather use an EASY-BAKE Oven than borrow my small-town dinosaur."

Bella picked up her tea but didn't drink it. Her hands turned white as she pressed them against the porcelain.

"My ovens—all of my equipment—are top of the line. Callan told me I was being ridiculous and to get over it."

Ahh. Supportive boyfriend one-oh-one: don't say get over it.

Still, Molly didn't think Bella was in any real trouble. "What happened after Trina joked with the officer?"

"She asked to see me and asked me about what Trina said. I didn't tell her about the visit. I told her I was just joking because who likes competition, right? But Georgie was working last night when I got back and she and Trina are friends."

Taking a deep breath, Molly let it out. She checked the time on her phone and realized she needed to get going. "Bella, I think you should tell the officer everything, just the way you told me. It's very unnerving to have a police offer question you for anything. If you explain that, you'll be fine. After all, you didn't hurt Skyler and the truth has a way of floating to the top."

The faraway look in Bella's eyes made Molly less sure of her own belief that the baker had nothing to do with the death of the celebrity chef. Molly waited a beat, hoping Bella would say, "You're right! The truth will come out and everything will be fine. After all, I did nothing wrong!"

But Bella remained quiet so long that Molly felt uncomfortable and far more unsettled than she had when she came. Which was saying something since she'd come from the scene of what was feeling a lot more like a murder than a possible suicide or accident.

"I need to go," Molly said.

Bella only nodded. She didn't stand to walk Molly out. She simply stayed seated, staring at nothing and leaving Molly with the sinking feeling that even with what she'd told her, Bella hadn't told her everything.

Chapter Nine

It didn't make sense, Molly thought as she drove the quiet roads home, the streets quieter than they had been for weeks. What would make the police think Bella was involved? If they didn't find out about the argument Bella had with Skyler, they were going off the simple fact that a beverage bearing the Morning Muffins logo was in the room. If there'd been a household brand name coffee cup in the room, would they have questioned those workers? Maybe Bella hadn't shared everything with her either, but Molly's gut told her the woman was no killer. *Right, because your gut is always on target?* Perhaps if it had been, she wouldn't have come home to her Lancaster apartment six months ago to find her boyfriend heating up her high thread count sheets with his ex-girlfriend. Molly didn't miss her ex, but she definitely questioned her own judgment. *Sam is completely different than any other guy you've known.* And, it was still early stages. She didn't have to pressure herself into defining feelings or anything else.

"It's the wedding," she muttered, turning on to Barker Street. The event was, literally, taking over the town, the people, the news, and Molly's own thoughts.

She pulled her Jeep into the gravel driveway, noting that there were several vehicles parked in the bed-and-breakfast's makeshift lot. Katherine didn't usually have so many guests at once so the five spots that were nicely paved alongside her shed weren't sufficient.

It would be another hot day in Britton Bay, even with the ocean breeze making it this far inland. The bed-and-breakfast sat far back at the top of a low hill, far enough from the beach to avoid the steady thrum of tourists, but close enough to walk. The white tents would provide a nice shade for the guests who were due to arrive Sunday for the late-morning wedding. Sunday. Providing it was still a go.

Molly got out of her vehicle and looked around, uncertain where to point her focus. Katherine was on the deck with the bride, her mother, and a few of the bridesmaids. Mini lanterns were being hung along the edges of the tents, which suggested the wedding was a go. An elevated 12x12 dance floor had been constructed under one of the tents and chairs had been set up to create an aisle that led to a sweet little spot under a magnolia tree. Molly wondered if, as a child, Patty had a tire swing hanging from that tree. Then she dismissed the thought, certain that the bride's mother had probably not been a playful child.

Molly was surprised when she turned and saw Calliope walking alongside Sam, down the front steps. She hurried through the various groups of people working on a variety of wedding-related chores to greet them.

Sam's smile was wide and instantaneous, making Molly's heart skip. Calliope's was just as wide and completely genuine. The red-headed owner of the Come 'n Get It Eatery was one of Molly's favorite people. The queen of gossip, she had a heart of gold, a backbone of steel, and knew more about Britton Bay than any database Molly could access.

"Hey, sweetie. How you doing?" Calliope pulled Molly into a tight hug and Sam winked at her from behind the cook slash owner slash mother-hen. The rib crushing embrace felt good. It soothed the shakiness inside of Molly that she hadn't even acknowledged.

"I'm good," she said, pulling back.

Calliope stepped to the side and Molly went to Sam, meeting him halfway when he leaned in to kiss her hello.

"Hey," he whispered.

"Hey. Your day okay?"

Sam nodded and brushed a hand down her hair in that way that made her feel like her friend's hug had. "I have to head into the shop for a bit. Calli was just dropping off some flyers for the bed-and-breakfast."

Molly remembered the coupon from last month's *Britton Bay Bulletin* in which Come 'n Get It Eatery offered fifty percent off the second meal. She'd suggested to Katherine and Calliope that they support each other by recommending one another at each of their establishments. So far, it was going well.

"Okay. Well, I'm actually going to ask around, see if anyone spoke to Skyler before...well, before," Molly said, looking down at the paved walkway.

"Thank goodness you didn't find this one," Calli said, squeezing Molly's shoulder.

She shuddered without meaning to and caught the look of concern in Sam's glance.

"I'm fine. I'll talk to you later?"

"Definitely. Stay safe."

He waved to both of them and they watched him walk the path, interrupt his mother and say his goodbyes.

"Good lord that man is a walking, talking, adorable temptation. He has no idea how sweet he is. Or how good-looking." Calliope crossed her arms over her ample chest and shook her head, side to side, while she continued to stare at Molly's boyfriend.

Molly laughed, looking at her friend with a mix of amusement and pride. "He really is."

Calli looped her arm through one of Molly's and squeezed her close. "Walk me to my car. How you holding up?"

Molly frowned. "Me? I'm fine. I feel horrible about another death in Britton Bay, but honestly, they haven't officially labeled it a murder." Though that made questioning Bella even stranger. *Didn't Bella say something about her mom and Patty not getting along years ago?* From what she'd seen and heard of the bride's mother, Patty wasn't missed when she left town, so it wasn't surprising that people were unhappy with her return. Or her over-the-top display of success via her daughter's special day.

"I heard it looked like foul play," Calli said, her tone more of a stage whisper than a polite muttering. A few heads turned their way and Molly waved to say hello with her free hand.

"I don't know who was there that could have told you that," Molly said. She hadn't seen any locals or regulars other than Corky. "Hey, do you know if the police brought Corky in at all?"

They walked along the side of the house that was edged by trees and away from the guests. Calliope had obviously parked on the street and there was a little path that led from a private sitting area to a white picket fence and gate.

"No. Do you know something I don't?"

Molly snorted. It wasn't likely. Or typical, but maybe today she did. "Corky found the body."

Her friend yanked her to a stop. "Shut the barn door!"

Molly laughed. "Front door."

"Whose front door? The hotel's?"

Happy that she could find laughter in this already off-putting day, Molly shook her head. "No. The expression is shut the *front* door."

Calliope's lips quirked up at the same time she shrugged her shoulders. "Oops. Well, neither door should be left open. But did he really? That poor man. I'm going to send Dean out to find him. I don't want him wandering too far off and getting himself all worked up."

Another car door slammed and Molly wondered how many more people could show up at this house. It wasn't even the wedding day. On Sunday, over one hundred guests were expected. The hotel in town was booked—though guests might not feel so comfortable with the current situation. She really should go check with Katherine and ask her some questions. Or better yet, the bride. Sam's cousin, Jill, stopped when she saw Calliope and Molly on the thin walkway. Again, Molly wondered about the conversation she and Sam had heard the night before. Skyler and the man she'd been speaking to would have been standing close to where she and Calli were now.

"I was hoping to sneak in and blend in with the crowd. Alan thought you might not want to be nosing around considering the close quarters and all," Jill said. She smiled at Calliope. "Hey, Calli. How's things?"

"Good enough." Calli dropped her voice a register and leaned into them. "Are you two investigating?"

Molly stiffened, Chris's warning clear in her mind. "No. That's for the police to do." She looked at Jill. "But if we can get some information, we can share it with the *Britton Bay Bulletin* readers before gossip starts working its roots into the ground."

Jill nodded enthusiastically, her short, blonde bob bouncing up and down. "What she said."

"What are you girls doing hiding in the bushes like this?" Katherine came down the stone steps that led from the backyard and parking area to where the women were standing. Molly frowned. Whoever Skyler had been talking to had taken those steps. *Unless Skyler went that way. But why would she? If she was walking back to the hotel, she would have gone through the front. Which means whoever took those steps is likely staying here.*

"Trying to get the scoop," Jill said, giving her aunt a hug.

Katherine hugged her niece back with enthusiasm and kept an arm around her waist even when she released her. "I'll say there's enough scoops to go around. My home and business have been turned into a prime-time soap opera."

Dark circles under Katherine's eyes suggested she was more stressed than she'd ever let them know.

"Is there anything we can do?" Molly asked.

Ever the optimist, Katherine smiled, and though it didn't have her typical zest, it was genuine. "They've got Madeline from the spa coming here with some of her girls to do manicures and pedicures. Chantel and her mother are not seeing eye to eye on where to go from here and Patty's gone off to her room."

"What are they arguing about?" Jill pursed her lips, showing her concern for her aunt.

"Patty wants to hire a new caterer, but Chantel just wants to get married. I think. Both of those women are on emotional roller coasters right now. I'm going to bring Patty up some tea and scones and see if I can help her smooth herself out."

Molly couldn't get over Katherine's generosity. It was there in spirit and action and made her want to do something special for her landlord as a show of appreciation. She'd have to think on it.

"Chantel wants to keep Skyler's staff?" Molly asked.

The idea that they'd just push forward made Molly wonder who would benefit from the celebrity chef's death. In truth, she couldn't imagine anyone wanting to be left with picking up where the revered—and feared—chef had left off. This was—despite Patty and Chantel's hopes—a small-town wedding. Lovely, no doubt, but it was hardly the gig to kill for. If, in fact, Skyler had been killed.

"She wants to move the wedding up actually. She doesn't want to stay longer than she has to." Katherine tucked one of her soft, brown tresses behind her ear.

"What's the groom say in all of this?" Calliope chimed in.

Katherine's phone buzzed and she turned it over in her hand, frowning. "We haven't seen him all morning. I need to deal with something. I'll see you ladies later. Calliope, thank you again for bringing the food. I'm going to devour that soup later today."

"Anytime, darlin'. Just make sure you eat it. You'll need your strength from the looks of things," Calli said, giving the B and B owner a quick, hard hug.

When Katherine strode away, Jill stared after her. "She runs herself so hard."

Molly smiled when Jill looked back at her. "I think she's okay, if that helps. This would stress anyone out and most days, she absolutely loves what she's doing here."

"And she's good at it. It's only a few days," Calliope said.

Those days would be tainted by the murder of the chef. Molly shivered. *Would the bride and groom think of it every time they celebrated or talked about their wedding?* She hoped not. Though it was tragic, she hoped that once everything was over, they'd hang onto the good. The sooner the death was resolved, the better it would be for the couple, Katherine, and the wedding party in general. *Especially if it was a murder.*

"You okay, sugar?" Calliope ran a hand up and down Molly's back.

"Yes. I just wish I knew if it had been a murder or suicide or just an accident, you know? I ran into Chris this morning and he didn't seem too inclined to talk to me."

Calli glanced around and then took a step forward so she was close enough Molly could smell her berry-scented lip balm. "I've got a cousin who works at the hospital. She's working today and I bet if we pop by there, we could find out what the death was ruled as."

Jill stepped closer. "Oh. That's a great idea. Molly, I can ask questions around here if you want to go do that and maybe we can meet back at the office and see if we can put together whatever details we can come up with."

It was a plan and having one gave her something to do besides worry and wonder. She nodded.

"Okay. Yes. Let's do that. We shouldn't be long. The hospital is about what? Twenty minutes from here?"

"Not even," said Calliope.

"Okay. Let's go. Jill, I'll text you when we're leaving there and will meet you back at the *Britton Bay Bulletin.*"

"Sounds good. Um..." Jill said, hesitating as she looked at both Molly and Calliope. "Maybe until we know what's what, you two stay safe, okay?"

Calliope laughed, but Molly nodded. She could still remember the feeling of being trapped with Vernon's murderer in her tiny cottage. The razor-sharp edge of fear with the paralyzing realization she only had herself to depend on. Molly squeezed Jill's arm.

"We promise. You, too."

Hopefully it was a promise they could keep.

Chapter Ten

While Calliope zipped onto the freeway to take them to the hospital, Molly did a little digging on her phone. She'd looked Skyler up on the internet already, but had stuck with news articles about success rather than social media. Right now, however, she wanted any access into the woman's life that she could get. The worry and fatigue etched in Katherine's lovely face haunted Molly's mind. She didn't need this strain when she was just realizing she could find her own happiness again. Not that Sam's mother was unhappy, but going out with the sheriff would be her first foray into the dating scene since her husband's passing.

"You're quiet," Calliope said, zooming into the left lane before she'd even flicked her signal switch.

Molly glanced up from the Facebook profile she'd found and gave her a tight smile. "I could say the same of you."

Calli waved a hand in her direction. "Dean hates when I chatter on while I'm driving. He says that's how we end up in the middle of nowhere. I say it's how we end up on an adventure, but we agree to disagree."

Molly smiled and continued to scroll through Skyler's uninteresting Facebook feed. Forty-seven friends, no posts in months. Then she had a thought. Skyler wasn't much older than Hannah. Maybe six or seven years? She texted Hannah quickly.

Molly: *What's your go-to social media app?*

Bubbles appeared immediately.

Hannah: *Snapchat, though I'm getting bored with it. I love Instagram. Guess I'm an old soul.*

Molly laughed out loud and Calliope looked in her direction. She held up her phone. "Hannah telling me that using Instagram makes her an old soul. Guess that makes me a dinosaur because I still prefer Facebook."

Calli shook her head and headed for the off-ramp. "You're still ahead of me. I like to talk with my mouth not my fingers so I guess I'm already one foot in the grave." She winced. "Sorry."

"It's okay," Molly said, knowing that her friend would never be disrespectful. Calliope was as full of love as Katherine was grace. Molly hadn't been sure where her adventure would land her when she'd decided to leave Lancaster, but she'd ended up in a great place, with amazing people.

Hannah: *Everything okay? You coming in soon? There's a lot of calls and our Twitter feed is busy.*

Blinking, Molly re-read the words. The *Britton Bay Bulletin* was not a strong presence on social media. It was Clay's job to establish the newspaper on the different outlets, but with Molly's arrival, his father's death…things hadn't happened yet. *So why now?*

She pulled up Twitter and saw that there were seventeen notifications tagging the *Britton Bay Bulletin.* Scrolling through, her stomach cramped. Skyler had tweeted the night before, asking her followers if they'd ever gotten themselves into something they thought they'd love, only to have it fall short of their expectations. *What on earth is that about?* It certainly seemed strange. Maybe it was a personal statement…a relationship? She thought again about the conversation she and Sam had overheard. That was ten-ish. Bella said the police had asked her whereabouts between midnight and six. But the tweet was after one a.m.

Her followers responded with hugs and hearts and several emojis. Skyler had tweeted them back until about one a.m. Then there was silence.

"Honey, we're here. You gonna look up from your phone?" Calliope had parked and was staring at her from the driver's seat. "You look like you've seen something awful."

Molly shook her head, tried to neutralize her expression. "I just…I don't know. I find it creepy and odd when people's social media exists after they…don't. People are still tweeting her. They have no idea she's gone and it feels strange."

Calliope turned off the ignition and reached over, squeezed Molly's hand. "Let's go see what my cousin can tell us."

They walked toward the front entrance of the hospital. Despite being one floor, it had several branches off of the main hub—the emergency room—that made it quite large. It serviced three different counties aside from Britton Bay. She'd driven past it on her trip into town but hadn't come this way since. The thick air made her wish she'd worn a tank top, though that was hardly appropriate work attire. Maybe she was just restless in her own skin.

They were almost at the doors when Molly spotted the male sous chef who worked for Skyler. He was leaning against a large cement column, wiping his eye with the heel of one hand while talking on the phone.

Molly grabbed Calliope's arm and steered her to the left so they could go around and not run into him. He hadn't spoken the night before, but if it was him Skyler had argued with, why would they have come to the bed-and-breakfast to argue? Katherine said they were finished with prep work around eight.

"What on earth—"

Molly cut her off. "Shh. He's one of Skyler's sous chefs. What's he doing here?" Molly's voice came out in a hoarse whisper. They rounded the other column and stayed behind it, probably looking ridiculous.

She could barely hear him as he sniffled and spoke to someone on the other end. "No. I don't know. We're staying to finish the job. How would I know? Well, it doesn't matter anyway. She ended things last night. Said it wouldn't work between us."

Wait...what? She *knew* she'd seen a look pass between them the night before.

"They won't let me see her. I just wanted to see her one more time."

His voice broke and sympathy pooled in Molly's chest. Until she thought about what he'd really said. *If Skyler had ended things between them, had he been mad enough to kill her over it? Had he argued with her? Threatened her? Was he who she tweeted about?* She needed to find out his name. Shouldn't be too hard. Katherine would have a record of it seeing as she liked to know who was in and out of her house and had a list of not only the wedding staff, but all of the guests. But who would kill someone and then go to the hospital to try to see them one last time? Her brain was starting to hurt.

You did this last time. You can't understand what goes through a killer's mind when YOU'RE NOT A KILLER.

"You okay?" Calliope squeezed her arm.

Molly's breathing was chopping in and out. She steadied it. Nodded. They stayed where they were, not speaking, barely breathing, until he hung up, looked around, staring up at the sky for a moment, and then walked away. He looked both ways as he crossed the roadway and kept going.

"Can we move now?" Calliope whispered.

"Yes. This just keeps getting weirder and weirder."

"I'll say. And I'm used to Corky so I know weird."

Molly managed a small smile, but immediately caught herself wondering if Corky was doing okay in all of this. She was more rattled than she should be and she hadn't even found the body this time. She hated the thought of the kind, but troubled man walking around with that image in his mind. *One worry at a time.*

They went through the sliding doors and Calliope led the way through a maze of hallways and corridors. The cafeteria was in the far back left corner of one of the wings. It bothered Molly when her stomach growled. *Someone had died. How could everything carry on as if no one had?* It was too philosophical a thought for that particular moment.

"What does your cousin do?" Molly remembered to ask right before they entered the cafeteria.

"Housekeeping."

Molly stopped. Calliope turned after a moment, realized she wasn't beside her and came back to stand in front of her.

"What is it?" Calli put both hands on her hips.

"How is your cousin going to help us with information if she's in housekeeping?" Molly figured that confidential information was probably tucked away in filing cabinets, accessed by nurses and doctors and health practitioners. She didn't want Calli's cousin sneaking around and getting herself in trouble on their—okay, *her*—behalf.

Calli smiled, looped her arm through Molly's and pulled her forward. "Oh, honey. Housekeepers are the invisible eyes and ears of all establishments. People tend to overlook them. Sure, they might say hello and have conversations, but their job is to move around quietly cleaning up after people without creating a disturbance. You'd be amazed at some of the things my cousin has found out just by being in the room."

Molly pursed her lips and thought about it. That definitely made sense. *Huh. Who would have thought?*

The cafeteria was large and very open. To the right was a buffet style serving center with four women behind it, serving up food to the few people in line. Though there was plenty of seating, few places were occupied. In one corner, a man and woman sat across from each other, their hands outstretched and clasped together across the table. A woman and a little girl, maybe about four or five, stood in front of a vending machine. The little girl looked like sunshine with boots. *Life just carries on.*

Calliope guided Molly to the table where a slender woman in Snoopy scrubs was reading a well-worn paperback, while nibbling on a carrot stick. She looked up when the two women approached the table and Molly immediately saw the resemblance in the bright blue, slightly mischievous eyes. She set her paperback down and stood.

"'Bout time you came to say hello," the woman said, pulling her cousin into a hug.

They rocked each other back and forth and the smile on Calli's face had Molly grinning. A single child from a small family, she'd never had large groups of people who wanted to enfold her in their arms and their lives. Until she'd come to Britton Bay.

"DeeDee, this is my good friend, Molly. Molly, this is my cousin DeeDee. Once she let's go of me, she's likely going to hug you next," Calliope warned with a laugh.

Her cousin did just that, giving an apologetic shrug. "I'm a hugger. Can't help it. Plus, I've heard about you and was looking forward to meeting you."

Molly returned the hug, which, thankfully, didn't last too long, seeing as, cousin or not, she didn't know the woman. She'd have to learn to relax a little with all of the affection if she wanted to become a true local.

"It's nice to meet you, too. Calliope always speaks so highly of her family and it makes me wish I had a big group to share all of the things you guys do."

Calli gave her cousin a gentle nudge. "I won't wreck her delusions by telling her how you used to pull my hair when we were little."

DeeDee smiled, completely unrepentant. "And I won't tell her you always deserved it."

They sat and DeeDee asked them if they wanted to grab anything from the cafeteria selection or the vending machine. Despite feeling hungry just moments ago, Molly's nerves felt like a coiled spring and she didn't want to chance it.

"I'm good. Thanks for telling Calli we could come talk to you about this."

DeeDee leaned in, pressing her hands flat on the tabletop. "I watched that competition, you know."

Molly had seen a few clips online, highlighting the final round of the cooking challenge, but she hadn't pressed play on any of them. *There's been no time.* Things were passing both too quickly and in slow motion. It was creating a vortex of surrealism in her mind, like she was walking through a thick fog.

"She won on a dessert, right?" Molly leaned in, mimicking DeeDee's posture. She was still an editor and knew how to gather facts and follow a story.

"She did. Some fancy macaron thingy—you know those little cookies that taste like sweet air?"

Okay. Hungry again. "I do. They're delicious."

"Well, hers took her straight to the finalist spot. Won a bunch of money, an ad in a food magazine and got lots of press for it. Small-town girl makes good. Who doesn't love that story, right?"

Molly smirked. Cleaner by day, storyteller by night. Calliope's cousin had the same flair for sharing a tale as Calli did herself. "Unfortunately it didn't have such a happy ending. I'm not trying to rush you, but were you able to find out anything about her cause of death?"

Calli had remained intently observant through their conversation, but she leaned in now. "Molly here figured out who killed Vernon. He worked at the *Britton Bay Bulletin* with her. You remember?"

"Of course I do. It was only a few months ago. Terrible that we have another murder close to home again."

Molly sat straight, her skin tingling with...anticipation? "Another? Can you confirm that Skyler's death wasn't an accident or self-induced?"

DeeDee glanced around the cafeteria. "I can't actually confirm anything, but what I can tell you is I was in the room when they brought the body in and there was nothing natural about the look of that girl. Something awful happened before she died and it wasn't peaceful." The woman shuddered and her brows scrunched together. "It was horrible to see. I don't know how anyone ever gets used to seeing things like that."

Molly couldn't imagine a job that entailed dealing with death on a regular basis, never mind staring it in the face. Literally. "How...what makes you think it wasn't peaceful?"

Calliope pressed a little closer to Molly and she felt the other woman's shiver. "Nothing too graphic. I don't need pictures in my head."

Again Molly thought of Corky and a shudder ran through her own body.

"She was all puffy and bloated. Like one of those blow up toys you hit and it comes back at you? You know those? She just didn't look...natural. I overheard the coroner saying he'd never known someone who worked with food to have so many food related allergies. Told his assistant—some kid from one of the colleges—that Skyler risked her life every day by surrounding herself with edible death traps."

Chapter Eleven

They didn't talk much as they walked back to Calliope's vehicle. Molly was on information overload. There were too many variables—too many people—to really get a handle on what the heck was going on. Sam had texted while they were chatting with DeeDee. So had Alan and Hannah. Molly needed to get to work. Hopefully Jill had found out something from her end and they could piece a few things together. She had a feeling Sam's cousin would want things sorted as soon as possible for her aunt's sake as well. *How is Chantel handling this? If she was already distraught this morning, this news can't be going over well.*

"You okay, sugar?" Calliope asked as they made their way back onto the freeway.

"It's just a lot. I'm not sure how to make sense of any of it."

"Thank goodness there's police for that then, right?"

There was a strong hint of suggestion in her tone, making Molly stare at her friend questioningly. "Didn't you ask earlier if we were investigating?"

Calli shuddered. "That was before DeeDee's description. Sounds nasty. I don't want you involved in something that'll end nasty. Leave things alone and let the professionals handle it."

She would. Molly had no desire to be smack dab in the middle of another murder investigation. But she also couldn't walk away from a puzzle. Especially one that had people she cared about on the fringes of it.

"I wonder if the bride and groom will still get married," Calliope mused.

Molly—who'd turned to stare out the window as the world whipped past—turned to look at Calli's profile.

"I hope so. I can see both sides of it. Everything is planned and set so I hope they do. But on the other hand, this is one heck of a stain on a very important day."

Calli nodded. "You're right. This is why I'm glad Dean and I didn't go for all of the pomp and circumstance, you know? We just needed each other and our families. Got married right at the end of the boardwalk as the sun set. The tourist season was over, we were in love, and the day was perfect. Wouldn't change a thing."

Molly leaned her head back against the cushion and sighed. "How'd you know Dean was the one?"

Calliope laughed. "The person you choose is the one. There's no magic formula, honey. Relationships, and marriage in particular, take work. You don't stay together because you're still so over the moon for each other, though I'll say Dean and I are and we're lucky for it, but we promised each other we'd stick it through. No matter what. We'd figure it out, the good and the bad and we'd be loyal and honest to each other always."

Interesting, Molly thought. Like a blend of fate and reason. Maybe something bigger than anyone could see pushed two people together, but they were responsible for keeping themselves that way. More than anything anyone else had said to her about love and forever after, Molly found comfort in these words. Because it made her feel like even though she might not have a choice about falling so hard for Sam, she *did* have a choice to make it work. To make it last.

"You want me to drop you at the newspaper or home?"

"I'd better head to work. We've got to get something in the paper quick. Once word gets around social media about Skyler, I have a feeling we'll have some extra visitors in town. Her 'tough girl makes good' story is still hot right now and her tragic ending is going to pull some of the big media outlets."

"I don't understand capitalizing on death. Would it hurt so much to spread some good cheer? To not always focus on the horrible things happening in the world?" Calliope rarely sounded jaded so her tone surprised Molly.

"It wouldn't hurt, no. It just wouldn't sell." Molly wasn't jaded either, but she knew how the world worked—or at least how news got sold. Though their intent had been to capitalize on the joy of the wedding and the tie between the past and the present. *We should still work with that.* It could be a sideline to what everyone would really be thinking about.

She gave Calliope a hug when her friend pulled up in front of the *Britton Bay Bulletin*. It was then she remembered Tigger and had a little flash of panic to go along with a tightening in her stomach. Poor guy. She'd given him no attention all day—just left him to his own devices. Before she entered the building, as she waved to Calli driving back toward the diner, she called Sam.

"Hey," he greeted. His voice eased the tension that ratcheted through her body. Soothed her like she'd slipped into a warm bath. *Oh, boy. You are so in trouble.*

"Hi. Are you at work?" She immediately gazed down the street toward Sam's shop.

"No. I'm back at my mom's. The cops showed up to interview everyone who interacted with the chef. They can't find one of the cooks and the bride and groom have been fighting loud enough to put on a show for everyone."

Molly closed her eyes on a sigh. "Your poor mom."

"She's handling it. *Brandon* is here so that's settling her nerves some."

Molly opened her eyes and her mouth quirked. "Sam."

"What?" She heard the little huff of air. Of irritation.

"She deserves to be happy."

"I know. Why are we talking on the phone? Come home so we can talk in person."

Her heart went into a spasm, jolting in her chest. *Come home.* What happened when she got too attached and things fell apart? Even people who were only days from pledging their eternal love to each other couldn't be sure things would work out in the end. Anything could happen. Who could be sure? For as long as she could remember, very few things in her life had ever stayed constant. She'd moved from state to state, sometimes country to country. They'd lived in over a dozen places by the time she was a teenager. Different schools, different friends. Nothing ever lasted. *Your parents did. Through all of that. And you and Tori are still close even though you've moved.*

"Molly," Sam said, his voice low.

There's no magic formula. Just like other areas of her life, the things that mattered to her, were worth the time she'd invested. She wasn't being fair to Sam or to herself by keeping a small piece of her heart on reserve. Just in case. So that if things went sideways, there might be something left.

"I have to work," she said. Then, standing on the sidewalk, with the sun beating down, she leapt. "But with it being so busy at the house, I wondered…maybe Tigger and I could stay at your place tonight?"

Silence rang through the phone like a siren. Deafening. Oh, God. She'd jumped too soon. He knew what she was asking. She hadn't just invited herself along to some event. She'd invited herself into his home. Further into his life. Overnight. And not because she needed comfort, which had been the reason for the one time he'd spent the night with her.

"That sounds great. That would be great. I...yes. Okay. Um. I'll see you later, then?"

His voice had gone a little high at the end, which pulled Molly out of her whirlwind of worries. She wasn't the only one caught up in the emotional storm and wondering whether or not to hold her breath and dive. She could hear it in his voice. He was scared, too. And being scared together, somehow felt safer than going it alone.

"Okay. Oh, I almost forgot. Could you let Tigger out and give him a treat while you're there? I've been gone all morning and I feel bad."

Sam chuckled. "Don't feel bad. He's been by my side since I got back here. I figured you wouldn't mind if he kept me company."

She didn't. She didn't mind at all. The fact that he'd naturally done so, including her pet in his activities was another push on her already wobbly heart. "Thank you. I'll see you tonight."

"I'm looking forward to it."

So was she. Or she would be, when she got her heart to beat at a reasonable speed again.

Chapter Twelve

After hanging up and taking a few deep breaths, Molly went through the front door of the *Britton Bay Bulletin*, the sound of the bell overhead making her smile. People walking in off the street were greeted with a small sitting area and a view of desks and partitions. Behind those less than attractive makeshift cubicles, the door to her office on the left and Alan's office on the right could be seen. The gray wall near the back of the mostly open room had a doorway into the small kitchen, staff area, and bathroom. On both sides of the doorway, old, framed editions of the *Britton Bay Bulletin* adorned the walls. The first issue ever printed was on there and sometimes Molly caught herself just staring at it, fascinated by the idea of one man starting up something that would impact so many lives. In the basement, the printing press took up all the room.

"Hey, Molly. How'd your morning go? I can't believe you had the misfortune of running into another crime scene." Elizabeth was coming around one of the partitions with a mug in her hands.

Molly felt an uncomfortable shiver. "It was eventful. I'm not sure what kind of scene it was. I don't think there's been a ruling on the death yet." She couldn't share what she'd learned just yet. She'd made Chris a promise, so for now, the information she'd collected would have to get stored away in a file labeled 'what the heck is going on?'

"Could be accidental, but from what I've heard about the chef, I wouldn't think so," Jill said, coming out of Alan's office, papers in hand. She gave Molly a pointed look, her eyes questioning.

Molly set her purse on Clay's desk, which was closest. He wasn't occupying it so there was no reason not to.

"Did you talk to anyone at your aunt's?" Molly needed to get a notebook and start jotting down what she'd found.

Elizabeth looked back and forth between the two women. "Oh, no. I see what's happening here. You two knock it off right this minute."

Frowning, Molly looked at her colleague and tried to figure out what she was talking about.

"What's the matter, Elizabeth?" Alan came out of his office, phone in hand. Dressed in a suit, as usual, his dark hair was graying at the sides, giving him a distinguished look. He reminded Molly a bit of her dad, though, even as a sergeant in the army, her father was far more relaxed than Alan ever appeared to be.

"These girls aren't thinking about reporting the news, Alan. They want to uncover it."

Alan gazed fondly at Elizabeth. She was best friends with Alan's wife and they were quite close. For a very brief period of time, after she'd started at the paper, Molly had speculated on *how* close they were. It was another reminder of how *off* her instincts could be, but she pushed that unwelcome thought deep down into her brain.

"It's important to dig to find the truth. If they happen upon something in the name of good writing, I'm sure they'll take it to the police."

Jill winked at Molly. "That's right, Elizabeth. Neither of us are looking to take down any perps."

Snickering at her television cop lingo, Molly picked up her purse and walked past the group of them. "We need to debrief about what we want to say. Give me ten minutes to get organized?"

"Sure thing, Boss," Jill said.

"Hey. That's my title," Alan teased.

"Nope. You're Big Boss."

Alan laughed and so did Molly. In her office, she stored her purse in the bottom drawer of her small, pine desk, then took a moment to center herself. A lot had happened in one morning. She looked around the nondescript, perfectly square office that she called hers and thought it was time to add a little personality to the place. She was staying. She knew this in a way she'd never known before. Molly had lived in enough towns, enough homes, to know that Britton Bay felt different. She hadn't been so sure when she'd arrived in town and certainly not after Vernon's death. But she felt like she was home. Here, at the bed-and-breakfast. In town. With Sam.

Pushing away all thoughts that induced belly fluttering, she wrote a list of what she wanted to know and what she did know. The 'what she knew' list was way too short. She wondered if Chris would be willing to talk to her yet or maybe one of the other officers. Molly texted Bella and asked how she was doing, then set her phone aside and opened her laptop. She typed Skyler's name into the search bar and began scrolling through. Who would want her dead? Her angry ex-lover who may or may not be the voice she heard the night before? Bella, for no solid reason Molly could think of? Murder tended to have basic motives. Money, revenge, love.

Molly clicked on a video of the cooking challenge that had been held in Skyler's hometown of Mabel Bay, Nevada. On screen, Skyler was rolling out a dough, nearly paper thin. Her angular face was hard and focused. She didn't glance up at the camera even though someone offscreen was asking her a question. The female sous chef who'd asked if everything was okay the night before came into view. She handed Skyler a small, dark bottle of liquid...maybe vanilla? They spoke under their breath and couldn't be heard before Skyler practically threw the liquid back at her sous chef. Anger flashed on the other woman's face for only seconds before she nodded her head and moved out of the frame. She returned a second later with a different bottle that looked the same to Molly.

When the screen moved to the host of the competition, Molly clicked stop. There were more videos to watch and lists to make. With any luck, before the wedding on Sunday, there would be some answers. For now, they'd focus on reporting only what they were sure of.

Jill and Alan were waiting for her near the large whiteboard she'd had installed along the wall outside of her office, off to the side of the cubicles. Elizabeth joined them a moment later, taking one of the stools and sitting in front. They often discussed stories, ideas, leads, and where they wanted to go with the various editions of the paper. Today, though, Molly had a different idea.

She wrote Skyler's name on the board and circled it.

"Are we going to go with her death rather than reporting on the wedding at all?" Elizabeth asked.

"I think we need to touch on all of it. Where's Clay?" Molly checked the clock on the wall. He should definitely be there.

Alan frowned. "Said he wasn't feeling well so I let him go home."

Clay didn't feel like a good fit for the paper, but it wasn't really Molly's job to point that out. She knew he was still dealing with the loss of his father, but he'd been a worse fit even before Vernon's death. Now, when they actually might need his assistance with the social media, he was not around.

"I can take over social media," Jill said, reading Molly's mind.

"Thank you. We need to get something on there. People are still commenting on Skyler's latest threads. She doesn't seem to use Facebook a whole lot, but I didn't get to check Instagram yet."

Jill made a note. "On it. So the wedding is still on?"

Molly wrote "Wedding?" on the board then drew lines extending from there and wrote the names or titles of the people staying at the bed-and-breakfast. The problem was, she didn't know either of the sous chefs' names or those of the bridal party. She frowned at the board.

"I'm not sure. As far as I know, everything is still a go. The last thing Katherine said was they were organizing the spa day to be at the house instead of in town."

She couldn't decide if she were in such a terrible position, if she'd choose to cancel or go ahead. On one hand, no one, other than who she'd shown up with, was close to the victim. Could they move forward without it hanging over their heads? She wasn't sure she could.

"I couldn't imagine marrying after this. How do you tell your wedding stories? Oh, once they cleared the bridal party of suspicion, we had a wonderful rehearsal dinner," Elizabeth said, her tone going up an octave as she imitated a bride.

Molly sighed. "Truthfully, I don't know if I could either."

Something—some thought or idea was stuck in the back of her brain, hiding under all of the other thoughts, just there enough to nag at her conscience.

Without really speaking to the people staring at her, she tried to voice her thoughts. "No one in the bridal party knew Skyler. But someone did. Someone knew her well enough to hurt her." Chantel didn't want Skyler there. Katherine had said that much, but so had the bride. She'd made it clear her mother was running the show and she wasn't enjoying it much.

"We don't actually know that someone hurt her. There's still the possibility that she died of natural causes or sadly, by her own hand. I think we should focus on the wedding. Mention the death but don't make it the main feature." Alan said. He rubbed a hand over his jaw, his eyes crinkled at the corners. He looked...perplexed. Which Molly understood since nothing felt settled in her mind either. But she knew, at least from what DeeDee had said, there was nothing natural about her death.

They talked about doing comparison photos of the bed-and-breakfast back when the bride's mother had lived there as a child and now, ready for her own child's wedding. Molly began to wonder if Chantel even wanted to get married in that home. She'd looked so sad this morning when Molly had stumbled upon her. Had she been angry as well? Another mystery. *Stick to your own job. Let the cops do theirs.*

After assigning jobs, Molly worked on the layout for a solid hour without getting completely distracted by her thoughts. When her stomach growled, breaking her out of the zone, she gave in. Checking with Alan to be sure he didn't need her there, she decided to head back to the bed-and-breakfast. After all, if they didn't find out more information, she'd have no stories to edit. Sufficiently convinced, Molly packed up her things and decided today was not a day for office work.

When she arrived at the house, there were fewer vehicles than the day before or even earlier that day. She didn't see Sam's truck, which likely meant he'd taken Tigger with him, either to work or to his home. She paused, mid-step and bit her lip, staring at the Victorian. Before she could decide on a plausible excuse for heading to the main house, the groom rushed out the back door and hammered down the steps. Shoving his hands into his hair, he cursed loudly before noticing Molly standing there in the middle of the driveway.

She couldn't tell whether it was rage or anguish or some terrible combination of both marring his features. The bride's mother came out, far calmer than he had, to join him. It only occurred to Molly, in that moment, that she hadn't seen the bride's father anywhere.

"You need to settle down, Blake. Maybe this is for the best," Patty said, her tone openly condescending.

Chantel and Blake. Sounds good together, I suppose. Neither of the guests seemed to care that she was standing there.

Blake whirled on his mother-in-law-to-be. "The best? You have no idea what's best for us. Everything is about you. Your childhood home, your dream wedding. Chantel didn't leave because of me. She left because she was tired of you trying to run the show."

He pointed at her, stepping closer, his face scrunched up in a way that perfectly matched the venom in his tone.

Molly tilted her head. "Um, sorry to interrupt, but what do you mean she left? Where did Chantel go?" Had she gone to speak to the police? Gone home? Or was she just getting some space to clear her head? Molly couldn't fault her for that.

Patty turned as if just noticing they had an audience. "You're the reporter. You work for Alan."

She sighed. "Editor actually. But yes, we met yesterday at the newspaper. Is Chantel all right?"

Blake dropped his hands at the same time Chantel's mother took a few steps closer to Molly. "How do you know my daughter?"

Why is this what matters? "I met her this morning while I was walking on the beach. She seemed upset."

Blake groaned. "God. I knew I shouldn't have let her go off on her own. I *knew it.*" He turned to look at Molly. "What did she say?"

It was difficult to gauge his expression. "Not much. We only chatted for a few seconds, but I know she came back here. And Katherine mentioned she and her bridesmaids were getting ready for manicures and pedicures."

Patty and Blake shared a look. Molly threw her hands up. "Simple question: is Chantel okay?" This wedding was turning out to be fodder for a *Twilight Zone* episode.

"You're a reporter?" Blake asked.

Molly stopped herself from rolling her eyes. Barely. "An editor. I work for the paper."

"But you must dig up stories? Find out things right? And you live here, in town?"

She hunched her shoulders up in a slow shrug. She didn't want to mention her living arrangements. "Yes."

He came nearer, his face so close she could smell the hint of cigarettes on his breath. "Chantel went missing about an hour ago. We thought she'd gone up for a nap, but she's gone. Please. The cops aren't taking it seriously. Someone needs to. Put an ad in your paper, show her picture, something. Anything. *Please, I'm begging you.*"

Molly's blood ran cold. She stared at him while feeling Patty's eyes watching them closely. Now she knew two things for sure: the bride-to-be was missing and the man who'd argued with Skyler the night before was the groom-to-be.

Chapter Thirteen

Molly's skin went cold despite the heat of the day. She stared at Blake and Patty, unsure of what to say or do. It was one of those suspended moments, like in the cartoons—everything stood still and in a second, a flurry of movement would create a whirlwind around them. Only, it didn't. The air was thick with more than the summer heat and when tires crunched along the gravel, their heads turned in unison to see the sheriff's cruiser pull up.

Katherine came out of the house, her mouth tight and here shoulders ramrod straight. She closed in on the group, coming up to Molly's side.

"Hi sweetie. You shouldn't be here in the middle of this," she said quietly, but took Molly's hands and squeezed, as though she needed the connection. The anchor. Molly's head spun. So the police had come to question everyone…had that included the bride? Why were there more questions mounting than answers?

She glared at Patty. "You are going to stop now. While you're paying to stay, this is my home and I understand it is a very stressful, trying time, but I won't have this continue. Clearly you and your son-in-law do not get along. One of you is going to have to find alternative accommodations if you can't work through your differences. If you feel the need to cancel the rest of your stay, I will refund you for the rest of the time, providing you see to it that all of the wedding preparations are taken down and dealt with. I simply won't have this kind of bickering and unrest in my home. You need to pull together instead of pointing fingers and assigning blame. I've asked the sheriff to join us," she stated.

Once again, Katherine impressed Molly. The woman was all class and pure strength. The sheriff wandered over, his long stride eating up the ground between them. Molly didn't miss the affectionate gaze he cast on Katherine before addressing the group. At over six feet tall, Brandon Saron was an imposing man, but it wasn't just because of his height. He had a face that could be gentle and compassionate but could easily turn hard like stone if he sensed injustice. He wore his own clothes, jeans and a pullover sweater, rather than his uniform.

"Molly. Nice to see you again." He stared at her a beat too long and she had to fight the urge to look down at her shoes or exclaim, "I didn't do anything!"

"Now folks, I am truly sorry for all of the upset surrounding what should be a wonderful occasion, but it sounds like there's a little too much tension. I think Katherine's suggestion that one of you find alternate accommodations is a good one. I'm sure we can work something out with the hotel."

"Where the chef was murdered? Are you crazy? That sounds like a fine idea if we want to be next," Blake said, shoving both hands in his pockets. Under his breath, not nearly quiet enough, he added, "Small-town cops."

Katherine closed her eyes and breathed deeply before scowling at Blake. Molly wasn't sure she'd ever seen Sam's mom scowl. Sheriff Saron crossed his arms over his chest.

"Seeing as this small-town cop knows about your misdemeanor assault charges, I'd be very careful about what you mutter under your breath, son."

Blake's eyes widened and Molly's heart sank into her stomach like a rock being tossed into the sea. He'd argued with Skyler, threatened her and he had a history of violence.

"God. I knew you weren't good enough for my daughter," Patty said, throwing her hands up in the air.

Blake's shoulders scrunched slightly, but he kept the sneer in place. "Those charges were dropped." He turned to watch Patty go. "Your daughter loves me and that drives you crazy. Too bad for you that only makes her want me more."

Patty didn't respond as she headed up the porch steps and made her way into the house.

Looking back at Molly, Blake pleaded with his eyes. "Can you help me find Chantel?"

"Molly," Sheriff Saron said, a warning clear as Waterford crystal in his tone.

Molly hoped the grin she gave him didn't resemble a grimace. "I'm staying out of it. I just came to see if Katherine needs anything and to get the names of the bridal party and caterers for the newspaper. We're doing a comparison on the house as it is now and as it was in Patty's day, but we thought we'd mention the wedding and try to keep the focus on that."

Sam's mom gave her a warm smile that clearly indicated she knew Molly was, at least partially, full of it.

"I'm glad to hear it. The last thing you need is to be caught up in another murder case," the sheriff said, glancing at Katherine.

Her heart beat against her ribs. "So, it is a murder?"

"When were you part of another murder?" Blake asked. Molly had forgotten for a second that he was even there.

"Old news. Sheriff?" She kept her gaze on the older, distinguished and handsome lawman. He and Katherine looked good together. The thought flitted in and out of her head and likewise, so did the hard tone of Blake's voice when he threatened Skyler. Was that somehow the reason for Chantel's sudden disappearance?

Looking at Blake, eager for him to be out of earshot, she kept her tone gentle and said, "There's another hotel if you're not comfortable staying at the closest one. It's just outside of town so you'll be plenty close."

Trying to keep the hope out of her voice so he didn't suspect her of wanting to speak to the sheriff about *him*, Molly added a smile to the suggestion.

Blake's lips puckered together in a pout. "Fine. I don't want to be here if Chantel isn't anyway."

He stormed off and Katherine stared after him longer than Molly. When their gazes met, she shook her head. "I thought having a wedding here would be wonderful. It never occurred to me that the entire event would be marred by tragedy."

Molly started to reach her hand toward Katherine's, but the sheriff beat her to it. He looked at Sam's mom with so much affection, Molly's breath caught in her lungs.

"No one could ever have predicted this, Katherine. It's not your fault." He looked at Molly, his gaze not nearly as gentle as when he looked at the woman he was clearly falling for.

"Are you on the record?"

Molly nearly scowled. It was like she was paparazzi in L.A. or something. "No. And *for the record,* not all journalists and reporters are slime. When the *Britton Bay Bulletin* provides information to Britton Bay, we want it to be factual and informative. It's not a tabloid. And I'm not even one of the writers." She hated the petulant tone in her voice. But, seriously, she cared about this place and these people, too, and she'd given no one any reason to think otherwise.

"Of course it's not, honey. Brandon wasn't suggesting that. I think everyone is just stressed." She eyed the sheriff, raising her brows and, not so subtly gestured to Molly with a nod of her head.

The sheriff sighed so heavily, Molly almost smiled. "I know you're good at what you do, Molly. I like you, which is why I'm going to tell you to stay out of this. You can go on the record with saying it is being ruled a homicide, but we do not feel the public is in any danger. You, however, with your tendency to snoop, need to be careful."

She felt like a child scolded by her father. It didn't help that she had to quell the urge to stomp her foot. "I do not snoop. But I thank you for the information. Katherine, is there anything you need? Anything I can do?"

Katherine shook her head, removing her hand from the sheriff's to rub her own arms briskly, despite the heat. "No. It's actually quiet right now. The bridesmaids are all in one room texting the bride nonstop. Chantel took off right after the pedicures. Blake should be packing up. I'm not sure where his groomsmen are, and Patty, well. Patty is Patty. Brandon, what about Chantel?"

He rubbed a hand over his face in such a naturally male gesture of frustration that Molly smiled. "She's probably just blowing off steam. We have no reason to be concerned yet. It's been less than two hours."

"Um, about that…the whole concern thing…" Molly stopped, pressing her lips together. Should she say it in front of Katherine?

Brandon straightened, going on alert. "What is it?"

"Last night, Sam and I heard someone arguing with Skyler. After speaking to Blake just now, I recognize the voice as his."

The sheriff—even thinking of him as *Brandon* seemed akin to calling teachers by their first names—put a hand to Katherine's shoulder. "Why don't you go in, honey. I'll be in shortly to make sure Blake heads on his way."

She nodded and smiled at Molly. When she left, Molly's worry flared. Even strong people could fall. "She's tired. Visibly. I've never seen her at less than one hundred and fifty percent."

He, too, watched Katherine go. "She's an incredible woman. She'll be okay." The tone of his voice suggested he'd make sure of it.

Looking back at Molly, his mouth in a tight line, he studied her just long enough to have her wanting to squirm. She stayed perfectly still.

"I'm letting the deputies handle this one unless they need me to step in. In particular, Officer Beatty is taking the lead. With my…uh, connection to Katherine, it seemed best. I'll need you to go talk to him and tell him what you told me. You're sure it was Blake?"

"Unfortunately, I'm positive." She put her hands in her pockets and rocked back on her heels. It was about the only thing she was positive about right now.

"What were they arguing about?"

Molly related the argument but cut herself off when Blake came stomping down the steps, a duffel bag thrown over his shoulder.

"Blake." Sheriff Saron's voice would have stopped anyone in their tracks, regardless of their name.

Blake looked over. "Yeah?"

"Why don't I take you over to the hotel? You don't have a car here, correct?"

Pursing his lips together, considering, Blake finally shook his head. "No. Thanks."

His gaze connected with Molly's and she saw something she hadn't expected to—a genuine concern. He loved Chantel. Whatever else could be said about him, true caring was hard to mask. She should know—she practically tap danced when she thought of Sam.

Molly nodded and Blake's eyes brightened. He might be the killer. It didn't feel right, but he was a definite suspect in her books. But she could look into a couple of things and see if there was somewhere close by Chantel might go. The police wouldn't take it seriously for another forty-six hours and by then…well, look what had happened in the last twenty-four. Besides, something about her just up and leaving felt strange.

As the sheriff and Blake turned to leave, Molly called the groom's name. He looked back at her and she did her best to ignore the weight of Saron's gaze. "Are all of Chantel's things still here?"

Blake shook his head. "No. That's why the cops won't do anything. They don't believe me that something happened. Like Patty, they think she just left me, but I'm telling you, she wouldn't." He looked at the house, like somehow it was responsible for everything. "She just wanted to get away from here. Not from me."

His glare didn't seem to concern Sheriff Saron. Molly didn't know what to say so she hung back and watched them go, a dozen thoughts colliding into each other making her brain hurt.

As she walked toward her cottage, another thought struck her: the male sous chef. And the female one. Where were they? So far, there was a murder, a missing bride, and two wayward chefs. Things were turning into more of a farce than a wedding and Molly worried that things were just getting started.

Chapter Fourteen

Molly pulled her portable whiteboard from her bedroom into the living room. She worked best in front of the fireplace because there was more room to pace. Plus, she could put some food out on the counter and snack while she worked. She dumped some salt and vinegar chips into a bowl, telling herself she'd eat healthy later. *You need to go to the police. The sheriff told you to. Since when do you buck authority? I'm not; I'm just getting my thoughts in order.*

At least, she was trying to. Jill or Elizabeth would handle putting together a story about the bed-and-breakfast. They might even be able to pull some archive pictures of it from years ago. They wouldn't have the story on her desk for editing for a bit yet, so she had some time. And a *lot* on her mind. She nearly smiled when she realized it was easier to think about the mystery spinning around her than the way Sam made her feel.

Pulling the cap off of a dry erase marker, she put Skyler's name in the middle of the board. What did she know? Off to the right of the board, she made a list.

1. Skyler argued with Blake.
2. Blake threatened Skyler around ten p.m. last night
3. Skyler tweeted at one a.m.
4. Chantel was crying at the beach this morning

She drew a line from the first item and put a note that Blake had a history of assault. She was almost positive that Sheriff Saron wouldn't want her to share that tidbit of information. *Speaking of information...*she'd looked up the other chefs' names. Kyle Wilks and Shannon Crombie.

1. Kyle was sleeping with Skyler
2. Skyler broke it off the night she died
3. Likely that Skyler died of unnatural causes
4. Police suspected Bella because of the take-out drink cup
5. DeeDee said the body looked bloated and puffy
6. Skyler had allergies—was she poisoned?
7. Death being ruled as a murder

The list was getting longer, but it wasn't helping her narrow down her thoughts on why Skyler would have been killed. She closed the cap on the marker, then tapped it against her chin. Walking back and forth in front of the board, she could admit that she was short on ideas. Her stomach growled again and she went back to the chips, grabbing a handful so she could nibble on them while she stared at her list. She couldn't decide if the wedding and the murder were actually connected or if the chef's death was just really poorly timed.

Okay. Skyler was possibly poisoned. With what? The food allergies! She wrote allergies beside Skyler's name. Did the police know about them? Most likely, if they were ruling it a homicide, they had an inkling of the cause of death. But did anyone else know? Had it been an accident or perfectly executed murder? *No outside ingredients.* Skyler wasn't friendly, but she clearly set parameters so people knew what she needed. She really did need to go speak to Chris. He might say something that would provide a clue as to why anyone would poison an award-winning cook. Surely, having a lousy attitude or a thousand-pound chip on her shoulder wasn't a reason to kill.

The police station was several blocks from Main Street, not too far from the high school and city hall. Several shops lined the street—a laundromat, convenience store, another bakery not nearly as good as Bella's, a thrift store and a few others. With its brick front, save the double glass doors, the police station blended well with the other buildings in the area. Like much of Britton Bay, it carried history in the weathering of the reddish brick, but the planters lining the steps and thirsty flowers spoke of recent care and attention to detail. Like much of the area, thickly treed areas surrounded them. She loved the fact that all of the buildings seemed to sort of grow out of the natural setting. Someone had worked hard to preserve the beauty of the landscape long ago and that tradition had stuck.

Pulling open one of the doors, she made her way into the reception area. She'd been here a few times before and the sensation of being back made her stomach tilt uncomfortably.

Molly recognized Priscilla, the front desk clerk. That was narrowing her job description quite a bit. Molly had learned that despite Britton Bay's growing population, staffing at the police department hadn't grown. While larger towns might have evidence rooms and labs, this one was basic. Behind the high counter, several desks were set together in twos, facing each other. It was quiet, with one officer leaning on the edge of a desk that butted up to another—a second officer was leaned back in a chair chatting with him.

"Hey Molly," Priscilla greeted. Her long, dark hair was tucked into a neat side braid and her clothing style was business casual.

"Hi Priscilla. How are you?" She rested her forearms on the counter, barely. It was a great divider between the front lobby and the police area.

"I'm good. Tired. We've all been pulling overtime. Between the murder and extra security for the wedding and the tourist season wrapping up, the paperwork is bananas."

Molly smiled, even though she felt bad for the woman. Who said bananas other than Gwen Stefani? "That's actually why I'm here. I need to speak to Officer Beatty."

Priscilla held her finger up when the phone rang. Molly waited for her to explain that to file a complaint, the caller needed to come down to the station. When she hung up the phone, she leaned over the desk and lowered her voice.

"Poor Corky is getting complaints all over the place. He's in a real state. I feel bad for him. He's harmless and he's one of our own, so why do people feel the need to call the police?"

Molly remembered how tortured Corky had seemed when she last saw him. "He's been through a lot. Have the police tried to speak to him about what he saw?"

Priscilla shook her head. The cop behind her gave a loud bark of laughter and then pushed off the desk, walking toward the other end of the room, away from them.

They didn't seem all that busy. Priscilla looked in the direction of the officer. "Mike is supposed to head out and bring him in. I guess he'll get to it when he does." There was a slight trace of rancor in her tone.

A thought struck Molly. "If you're putting in extra hours, do they have you covering extra duties as well?"

"Always. Busy or not, I run the front desk, help with evidence, process fines, file complaints." Priscilla pasted a smile on her face, but Molly saw past it to the fatigue.

"Wow. I guess it makes the day go by fast if you're so busy. Are you processing evidence for the Friessen case?" It was probably too much to hope for a little peek at what was included.

Priscilla straightened, as though Molly's question had reminded her that she was on the clock and a public official, of sorts. "Yes. You wanted to speak to Officer Beatty about the case? He's not here right now. He's been on the go all day. I can leave him a message to get in touch with you."

Recognizing the barrier that had just sprung up between them, Molly tried not to push her luck. She didn't need to alienate anyone with her nosiness. *Curiosity.* Nosey sounded too... busybody.

"That would be great. I have some information about Blake, the groom. I'm heading over to Sam's in a bit, but he can reach me on my cell."

The receptionist's face softened. "How's that going?"

Molly lowered her arms to her sides. "Great. Things are really good."

"I'm glad to hear it."

Knowing when to retreat, Molly smiled. "I should get going. Thanks for passing on the message to Officer Beatty."

"No problem. Just one of my many jobs."

As Molly headed back out into the heat, she thought about Priscilla's many hats. If one of them was processing evidence, perhaps she'd have some insight into what was collected at the scene. What could have possibly poisoned Skyler? Molly couldn't wrap her head around the idea that Bella had added something to the latte she'd delivered. Yes, she'd seemed almost more withdrawn after talking to Molly than when she'd arrived, but it was harder to believe Bella would hurt someone than it was Corky. It just didn't fit. Priscilla made it clear that she wouldn't share information though. Or, maybe, she didn't want to talk at work, which made sense.

Like many other Britton Bay natives, Priscilla was probably no stranger to sharing a little insider knowledge in the right setting. What was the right setting? She thought of Calli's easy ability to get people to unload all of their secrets and an idea formed. If she could get Bella, Priscilla, Calli, and maybe a few others together for a girls' night, it would seem friendly, normal, and might fill in some of the gaping holes in Molly's knowledge. Even if it didn't provide answers, it would be fun. And the whole town could use a little fun right now.

Chapter Fifteen

Molly stood outside Sam's apartment building a full hour early. *By the time you actually ring him, you'll be right on time.* She didn't know why she was frozen in front of the double glass doors. Her reflection showed a normal, fairly attractive woman approaching thirty. *Normal. Ha!* Nothing inside of her felt normal. At this point, she was beginning to wonder if she knew what *normal* was.

She was worrying and stressing about crossing a threshold with her extremely kind, funny, charming, and very sexy boyfriend whom she'd been dating for over two months. She'd been in adult relationships before and knew the natural progression of them. Heck, this was the longest she'd ever held back on…progressing. But that freaked her out even more because she knew there were two reasons. One, she was scared she'd end up hurt and two, she knew Sam mattered more than any of the others had. He was what people meant when they said *you'll just know.* If she let herself indulge in thoughts of him, she knew she'd have to face the fact that she was more than a little enamored with him. It felt too quick, but it also felt right.

Stop. Stop. Live right now. This minute. Some people didn't get to do even that and just thinking that terrible thought set her in motion. She buzzed his number.

"Hello?" His voice made her smile.

"Hey. I'm early." *Duh. Nice start Captain Obvious.* She gripped the strap of her overnight bag a little tighter.

"Molly?"

Who else? Had his voice squeaked? "Um, yes."

"You're early." The speaker crackled.

Nerves pounded on her rib cage. No gentle fluttering or awakening, they were jumping up and down. It took effort to keep her breathing even. "I am. Is that...all right?"

There was a pause. A notable pause. "Why don't I come down?"

Why would he come down? She buzzed back to ask but he didn't answer. He didn't want her in his apartment. Nausea slid along the lining of her stomach, a snake slithering and burrowing into a nest of panic. She'd told herself not to fall. Hadn't she held back just a little for this exact reason? In seconds, Sam was coming toward the glass doors, a nervous smile on his handsome face.

He pushed open the door, but Molly stayed rooted to the spot. She couldn't move.

His grin was lopsided. "Hi. I wasn't expecting you for a bit."

She stared at him. Little pieces of her—pockets she'd tucked away—had known when her ex was cheating. She didn't face it until she'd had no choice, but after the fact, she knew that she *knew.* Why she'd ignored her instincts, she couldn't say. But Molly didn't sense that with Sam. He was loyal. Genuine. Real. He loved his mother. He worked hard and was well loved by the people of Britton Bay. He took care of her dog without her even asking. He was a *good* man. Like his father had been before him. And clearly, he was hiding something.

"What's going on?" She put her hand on the door, something to hold onto as she breathed through the pain in her chest.

"What do you mean?" Again with the break in his voice. His brows went up too far when he asked.

Weren't people supposed to learn from their mistakes? Why couldn't she? *You have faulty judgment. You always have.*

"Molly?"

Tears burned and that made her mad. She shook her head, started to back away. "I can't do this."

Turning, she walked back toward her Jeep, her steps too slow to match the pace of her heart. Sam was beside her in an instant and then in front of her, walking backwards so he was facing her.

"Hey. Wait, what's going on? Where are you going?" He held her shoulders, stopping her in her tracks. Her eyes burned. Her stomach burned and she couldn't look at him. She stiffened her body, like somehow that would block the blow of anything he said.

Sam lifted her chin. The spot where his fingers touched her skin blazed. Allowing herself to blink once, Molly then worked to keep her eyes as wide as possible. That way tears wouldn't fall.

"Molly," Sam said. His voice was hushed and rough. He bent his knees to search her eyes. She looked away with just her eyes.

"I'm early. I've clearly interrupted something." She was grateful that her voice was steady.

He knew her history. That's how relationships worked. Go on a couple of dates, fall a little, share your skeletons, maybe some more falling. He didn't have the same scars as her, but he knew hers.

Sam put both hands back on her shoulders, squeezing, almost reassuring. He waited until she was looking at him—really seeing him before he spoke. "Not that. Never that. I'm not your past, Molly. I'm right here and now and when you're ready, when you stop being so scared, I fully plan on being your future. You should know that. You're all I see. All I want. I wouldn't jeopardize that for anything."

Molly shook her head, afraid to believe him. He had her pegged there. "You don't want me to come in. Obviously, there's a reason."

He nodded. "There is. A few actually. And not one of them is what you immediately thought. That'll never happen. I know it's hard for you to trust that, but I swear to you, it'll never be something you have to worry about."

Molly saw and heard the hurt behind the statement. It was unfair to paint him with a brush that so clearly didn't suit him. She knew that. She felt it all the way through, had from the first time she'd met him, that she could trust him. It was herself she didn't trust.

"I'm sorry," she whispered.

Sam leaned in, kissed her forehead. "I know."

Her fingers felt frozen at her sides and her mind and heart didn't quite know what to do, what to think.

"I wanted to surprise you by giving Tigger a bath and a trim. I figured, how hard could it be. He and I were going to show you how nicely we cleaned up," Sam said, a hint of a smile landing on his lips.

Air whooshed out of her lungs in a sort of laugh. "You and Tigger?"

Nodding, he gentled his fingers, turning her so they were headed back toward his apartment. His arm around her shoulder, her body tight to his side, she felt surrounded. Protected and cared for.

"Things didn't go as planned. As you know, Tigger is a bit...bouncy. Let's just say he more bathed me than I did him. My place was a mess, I had your wet dog who still needed a trim and the rest of the soap scrubbed out of his ears. I wanted to cook for you and everything was falling apart."

They stopped in front of the building and he turned her to face him again. Her heart was growing in her chest, puffing up like a balloon.

"That all sounds very sweet." Her voice wobbled.

He shrugged, then winced. "It might have been. But, in the end, I called Jill. She took Tigger to the groomer for me. I figured food was more important so I got started on dinner—after I cleaned myself up. But, well, my apartment is still kind of...damp."

Molly laughed. "Damp?"

Sam groaned. "Tigger is pretty slippery when he's wet. He managed to pounce on my couch and all over my floors pretty good before I got him wrapped in a towel."

More laughter bubbled up as she pictured Sam trying to wrangle her wet, soapy dog.

"So, you don't want me to come up because your place isn't clean? And the reason it isn't clean is because of my dog?"

A soft pink darkened Sam's cheeks and Molly pressed her hands to his face, cupping his cheeks like he often did hers. Before he could answer, she went up on tiptoes to kiss him.

Against his mouth, she pulled back only enough to whisper, "That might be the sweetest thing ever."

Sam chuckled and one of his hands wove into her hair. "I'm glad you think so because now that you're here early, you get to help with either clean up or cooking. Jill should be back with Tigger in a couple of hours. There's a groomer about twenty minutes from here and she was able to sweet-talk her way into an appointment, but apparently it takes a bit. Now I sort of see why."

Molly's heart raced and melted at the same time. In a world full of crazy, he was her calm. Maybe she was scared, but she'd rather be scared with him than without.

Leaning in, she kissed him once more, taking her time. He'd clearly showered—again. The scent of his soap and aftershave tangled with her senses making her crave a closeness she'd denied herself as a way to protect her heart. But it was too late. He already possessed it.

One of Sam's hands went to her hips, squeezed there and pulled her closer. She sighed into his mouth, trying to tell him, *show him,* what she felt. Not that she could put it into words just yet or label it. But it was big and intense and a bit terrifying. The flip side of those feelings were exhilarating. And incredibly freeing.

"Molly," Sam whispered, his breath ragged as he pressed his forehead to hers.

"Sam." They stared at each other and she wondered if it was just her heart beating fast.

"We can go in."

She nodded, her forehead still against his. She smiled at him, anticipation thrumming through her blood. "We should."

"You want clean up or food?" They still didn't move.

"Neither," she whispered. "I think they can both wait."

His eyes widened and she ran a hand down his arm, found his fingers and locked her own inside of his strong ones. Sam dug his keys out of his pocket with his free hand and opened the door. They walked to the elevator in silence. When the doors slid shut, she smiled again before she moved into him. He was ready. Waiting. His arms went around her waist, hers around his neck and he lifted her just a little as his mouth covered hers.

Molly leaned her head back, loving the sound of Sam's uneven breath. "One question."

"Hmm?" He nuzzled the side of her neck, sending shivers over her skin.

"Did Tigger jump on your bed after his bath?"

Sam looked at her, his eyes dancing with amusement. "Nope. He steered clear of the bed."

Molly kissed him again. "Good dog."

Chapter Sixteen

Molly smiled the whole time she diced vegetables for the salad they'd have with Sam's BBQ burgers. There was a sweet, gentle hum in the air, making her feel warm and incredibly cared for. Sam chatted about his upcoming jobs and the car show he was working to sponsor. He had a thing for classic cars and knew several clients in many counties that owned them. She thought again of the tin signs and wondered about having one made for him. They were unique and special. Like him.

They avoided conversation about the wedding and the murder. It was light and fun with a side of romantic, moving around his kitchen and feeling so welcome in his space. His life. And she knew, as a shiver ran down her body, in his heart.

They were setting the table when the door chimer buzzed. Sam pressed the button and Jill's voice rang through.

"Delivery. Adorable, bouncy, and clean dog."

Sam smiled, buzzed her in and turned back to Molly. "I can finish up the salad. You've already had to do too much. Next time, I won't try to multitask and I'll make the whole dinner myself."

She loved that he wanted to do that for her. She also liked putting together a meal with him. "I could also cook for you, but I think our relationship needs more time before we deal with that hurdle."

Sam's laughter was deep and infectious. "Come on, give yourself a break. You've made me food. There was those grilled cheese sandwiches."

Molly set the knife down. "I burnt them."

"A little. But what about the soup and biscuits. That was good."

She grinned. "You're being very sweet, but canned soup and biscuits from Bella don't count."

He nodded gravely. "You're right. We'll take it slow."

He was still by the door when Jill knocked and the second he opened it, Tigger burst through. Molly came around the counter that separated the living and kitchen areas and knelt down to greet him. He smelled great, which he obviously wanted her to know because he practically climbed into her nose.

"Okay, okay. I'm happy to see you, too. Oh, my goodness." Laughing, she fell back onto her butt and rubbed him, earning furious tail wags. He whimpered, like he couldn't contain all the joy inside of him.

"I need someone to be that happy to see me," Jill commented, shutting the door behind her.

"Get a dog," Sam suggested, grinning at his cousin.

Jill poked him in the shoulder. "Mr. Funny-Guy." Walking further into the living area, she peered over Molly and looked at the counter. "Mmm, burgers. I like homemade burgers."

Molly spoke without thinking. "Join us. Sam thinks I have the appetite of four people so there's definitely enough."

She caught his gaze and realized she should have run that by him first, but he just smiled and then looked at Jill. "Do not get between Molly and a box of cookies."

Jill laughed and leaned closer to Sam, using a stage whisper. "I work with her. I know."

Tigger left Molly's lap to run over to Sam, who crouched and gave him some attention.

"I'll just run to my car. I left my purse in there because I didn't think I was staying," Jill said, heading for the door.

"No pressure if you can't," Sam said, his voice teasing.

"I won't overstay my welcome. I just want free food that doesn't come in a take-out container." She winked at Molly and grabbed Sam's keys from the bowl that sat on the little side table by his door. "Be right back."

Sam stood and came over to Molly, holding out a hand. She took it and when he pulled her up, didn't mind one bit when he yanked her against him for a hard, but sweet kiss. Pulling back, he brushed her hair off of her face. Tigger found a chew toy and started gnawing on it.

"Sorry the females in my family seem to like crashing our dinners," he said, staring down at her with an intensity that both thrilled and alarmed her. Though, the alarm was less than it had been earlier. She needed to stop being so afraid to live her life. And that meant letting herself fall. *Like you have a choice on that one.*

"It doesn't bother me. At all. I love being alone with you and the time we spend together. But I really like your family, too. Your mom is lovely and Jill is great."

He nodded, looking reluctant to agree. "I guess. But I think I like the alone time more than you do."

Going up on tiptoes, she wrapped her arms tighter around him. "I don't think that's possible. But, unlike you, I didn't grow up in a big family. I always envied friends who were never lonely because they could hang out with cousins or tell secrets to a favorite aunt."

Sam's face softened and he stroked her hair again. "I don't like the idea of you ever being lonely."

Heart thumping hard, she kissed him gently. "I'm not anymore. But I like people. You know that. Maybe if you hadn't had so much family you'd…"

Molly broke off, her thoughts stumbling. Jill came back in and Sam continued to stare at her.

"You okay?"

She nodded, dropped to her flat feet. "I am, but…" But what? Her brain was grasping at something.

"Everything all right?" Jill asked, coming into view.

"Molly was just telling me how much she likes me *and* my annoying cousin, but then she stopped, so I think she changed her mind." He loosened his grip on her and pointed at Jill. "I blame you."

Swatting his chest and stepping back, she laughed. "Stop it. That's not it. I was just thinking about family and having someone to turn to."

"You're close to your parents, aren't you?" Jill settled into the corner of Sam's couch.

Molly shook her head. She wasn't making herself clear. "Yes. I am. But that's not what I'm thinking about. If Chantel's mother grew up here and she has family here, then there's a good chance she might have turned to one of them."

"The bride?" Jill looked up at Molly who'd started to pace.

"What's going on with the bride?" Sam went back to the kitchen and picked up the plate of burgers from the counter.

Molly spun around to face him. She hadn't talked to him about it. She'd brainstormed, gone to the station, and then…and *then* she'd been too caught up in him to think about the bride or anyone else.

"She's missing."

"What?" Sam and Jill spoke in unison.

Molly turned so she was sort of facing both of them, took a deep breath, trying to get her thoughts to slow down so her words could catch up. Sam held the burgers in one hand, waiting, and Jill perched on the edge of his couch. She told them what had happened when she'd arrived at the bed-and-breakfast.

"So, it was him who threatened the chef?" Sam asked.

Jill put her hands up, her face scrunched in concern. "Wait, he has a history of assault? Are the police looking into him as a suspect?"

"I don't know. The sheriff was giving him a ride to a motel on the other side of Britton Bay. Blake didn't want to stay at the hotel."

"Don't really blame him," Jill remarked.

"I'm sure *Brandon* worked it that way to give the groom a thorough but subtle grilling on the ride," Sam said.

Jill's brows popped up. *"Brandon?"*

Sam shook his head and glanced at Molly. "I need to put these on. Be right back." He walked through the kitchen and slid open the patio door.

"What's up with him?" Jill pushed back in her seat, bringing her legs up to sit crisscross.

"Katherine and the sheriff are dating," Molly said.

Jill's expression softened, her eyes going warm. "Aw. That's hard on Sam, but good for my aunt. She's a vibrant woman. And the sheriff is a great match for her."

Molly glanced toward the kitchen then back at Jill. "I think it reminds him, even though he didn't need the reminder, that his dad is gone."

Nodding, Jill sighed. "He was a good man. Impossible to replace. But, she deserves to move on."

They said nothing for a moment, then Sam came back in and put the plate in the dishwasher before joining them. He sat in the chair, close enough to Molly that he reached across and took her hand.

"So, the bride? Sam prompted.

It distracted her a moment, the way his fingers linked so naturally with hers. She looked at their joined hands and smiled. He squeezed gently.

"I was thinking that maybe she went to an aunt or cousin here in town. If she did, she's not really missing. She's just hiding out."

"I'd hide out, too," Jill said.

Sam and Molly both looked at her, waiting for her to continue. "Her wedding has turned into a zoo. Heck, it started as a zoo. Now, there's the death and I just don't know if I could work around that. If I could put it out of my head and carry on."

"Truthfully, neither could I. I saw Chantel crying on the beach this morning. She was really upset."

"Did she say why?" Jill fidgeted with her purse and then pulled out a pad of paper and a pen.

"I'm not giving interviews right now," Sam said, making both women smile.

"I need to write some of this down," Jill said.

Molly curled her legs up under her and Sam pulled his hand from hers. When he stood up, he leaned down and kissed the top of her head. "I need to check the burgers."

She watched him walk away and turned back to Jill only when the woman huffed out a breath.

"What?" Molly asked.

"I can't decide which of you is more smitten," Jill said, smiling.

"I'm okay with a tie." Molly angled her body to face Jill. "I did the same thing at home, wrote everything down. To me, Blake and Kyle are the most likely suspects. Blake has the assault thing, plus he was arguing with her. Kyle was upset about Skyler, but he was angry, too. Also, I don't know if he actually went back to the bed-and-breakfast. Chantel basically said her mother is making this more about her than what Chantel wants. Blake said the same. Did you know, Chantel didn't even choose her own bridesmaids?"

Jill scowled and jotted notes down. "What do you think Skyler and Blake argued about?"

The sliding door shut and Sam came back in. "About five more minutes."

"It sounded pretty personal and she said that he'd begged her before," Molly remarked, looking at Sam for confirmation.

"Definitely personal. My guess is they hooked up and he didn't want his bride-to-be to know."

Sam perched on the arm of the chair and Tigger, who'd been dozing, jumped up and came over to him, going up on hind legs to get Sam's attention. "Hey, bud. Good nap?"

Molly smiled. Her two guys. They were both cuties and she wasn't sure what she'd do without them. She thought of how she'd felt when she showed up and misunderstood Sam's response. Hurt. She'd wanted to flee.

"Maybe Chantel did find out. That could be why she was crying and more importantly, why she left," Molly said.

Jill stopped writing. "You said that Skyler died of unnatural causes. Bella said they suspected it was something she ate or drank, which is why they questioned her on the latte cup. So, if they argued, he went back to his room and decided to go out, maybe he didn't tell Chantel why, confronted

Skyler at the hotel and killed her. Maybe he couldn't account for where he was when he got back, hence the fight that sent her to the beach in tears."

It took Molly a second to realize what Jill had said. "Bella talked to you?"

Jill nodded. "She called this afternoon. Said she spoke to you, too, but wanted my thoughts on talking to the police."

It made sense. Jill had been gone a while, but she'd grown up here and was friends with everyone. Why had Bella turned to Molly in the first place then, instead of a trusted friend? Probably because Molly had found out the truth about Vernon's killer. That seemed to color everyone's opinion of her in different ways.

Jill bit the end of her pen, then tapped it on the paper. "But what did he poison her with and was it intentional?"

"Hold on," Molly said. "Skyler was tweeting at one in the morning. We need to find out if Blake was with Chantel at that time. If he was, then it wasn't him."

"Which means we need to find Chantel," Jill said.

"Or, we could let the police do their jobs because they have all that training and the guns," Sam offered, standing again.

Tigger followed him when he went to the patio door. "Grab yourself a plate, Jill. Burgers are done. Be right back."

The conversation shifted to other things during dinner, which was a bit of a relief. Molly's brain felt like it might combust with all of the unanswered questions, but Sam was right. The police would do their jobs. It was one thing to want details for accurate reporting, but another to insert herself into a situation that had nothing to do with her. She just hoped the curiosity would wane. Or the case would be solved. That would work, too.

They were just wrapping up dinner when Molly's phone rang. Excusing herself from the table, she found the phone in her purse and answered.

"Hey, Molly. It's Chris. I heard you were at the station. Sorry I didn't get back to you earlier, but I was wondering if you could come down and give your statement."

Molly glanced at Sam and Jill who were watching her. "Right now?"

"It would be better for us to get it done."

The curiosity leaped up like Tigger did for his treats. Before she could think of a way to get a little more information out of him, he gave her another carrot.

"We've got Blake in custody and I'd like to hold him as long as I can. It'll be easier if I have your signed statement about what you overheard. Sam's too, actually."

"We're on our way."

Chapter Seventeen

Sam insisted on driving them to the station. Jill took Tigger with her, heading back to the *Britton Bay Bulletin* to update the information they had online. Molly asked her to mention on their Facebook page that if anyone is in contact with Chantel, could they please message the paper. It didn't step on police toes—technically—since they didn't say she was missing. But it would help put Blake's mind at ease that something was being done. *Unless, you're being a fool and Blake is responsible for not only the chef's death, but the disappearance of his bride.*

"You okay?" Sam took Molly's hand across the console. The sun had set and now the sky was a smoky shade of blue. Mountains surrounded them, giving a sense of protection. This peaceful, blissful little town that had Molly facing more murder in three months than she'd come across in her whole life.

She looked at his profile and tried to shake off her dark thoughts. "I am. I just don't know what to believe or how to make sense of it."

There was a bit of traffic heading to the station. Tourists were on their way out or enjoying final days, which meant the streets were crowded.

"Why do you feel like it's your job?" His tone was gentle and inquisitive.

Resting her head back on the headrest, she thought about the question. "I guess I've always wanted to know the why of things. How things work, why they end up one way over another. Human nature is such a versatile thing—how we all look at one situation in a dozen different ways. So there's that, just the human interest piece. But I think part of it is because I've been hurt and I feel like I've let that happen in my life by not digging below the surface. Somehow, it's easier to not put up with surface level answers for someone else than it ever was for myself."

Sam parked in front of the brick building Molly was, once again, frequenting too often. When he shut off the car, he turned in his seat.

"I think it's also human nature—self-preservation, really, to not dig too deep when we know we won't like the answers. For ourselves I mean. You could look at your refusal to look further as you being the kind of person who wants to believe the best."

She unhooked her seat belt and leaned in for a kiss. She rested her head on his shoulder for a brief second. "I like that you think so."

His hand came to her arm and squeezed. "You know I'd never hurt you, right? You can dig as deep as you want. The only thing you'll find is that every day I care about you more."

Tears blurred her vision and she blamed fatigue. Emotion. Tension. All of it together.

"I know," she whispered back.

They let the moment slip away, but she felt stronger because of it. They walked hand in hand into the police station. A gentle breeze had dropped into the air sending the scent of the ocean and wildflowers swirling around them. She was coming to love this town and hated the tragedies marring its welcoming vibe. The reception area was quiet, making it feel like their footsteps echoed on the linoleum. Probably just her imagination, but it seemed darker, more ominous, with no one at the front desk. There wasn't even the hum of chatter or keyboards clacking.

They weren't even to the counter when Chris came out of one of the offices.

Molly smiled. "It's like you're psychic. You just knew we were here."

His low chuckle sounded tired and it matched the creases around his eyes. "I probably shouldn't wreck your illusions and tell you footsteps echo more than a voice off a cliff in that lobby."

Sam nudged her with his hip. "They might even have some surveillance cameras rigged up."

Now Chris gave a full-bodied laugh. "Top of the line for Britton Bay PD." He opened the half gate and moved aside so they could come behind the counter.

"Thanks for coming in," Chris said.

"Getting lonely and bored all by yourself," Sam asked.

Chris shot his friend a look and ignored him. He led them to the office he'd come out of and gestured for Sam and Molly to sit on one side of the table. A camera was set up in the corner of the room. Several pads of paper and pens littered one section of the long rectangular surface. Chris took a seat, picked up a pen, and pulled one of the pads toward him. He wrote the date and Molly's name then passed the tools to her while he opened the laptop that sat there.

"You write your statement down, but I'm going to have you read it to me when you're done. That way, if you've forgotten anything, reading it back might jog your memory."

He pressed a couple of keys on the keyboard then looked at Sam. "You overheard Mr. Findle as well?"

Findle? That was his last name? It almost made Molly smile. They seemed so perfect—the storybook, soap-opera named couple. Blake and Chantel. Findle. Perfection was a myth—something people believed existed, strived to achieve. Skim away the top layer and real life shimmered for everyone. It was almost comforting.

"I did," Sam replied.

Chris readied a pad for him as well and gave the same instruction. They both spent a few moments writing down exactly what they'd heard the night before Skyler's death. When they read the statements back, Molly's mind churned with unanswered questions. *Yes, he threatened Skyler, but the desire to save Chantel from learning something that would hurt her was real. The pain she'd seen in his eyes when he talked about Chantel being gone, was real. Just like the tears Chantel shed on the beach were real.*

"Molly?" Chris stopped typing and she realized she'd lost focus.

"Hmm?"

"Can you remember anything else?" His eyes bore into hers. He knew she had a good memory for this sort of thing. He didn't always like it, but there were times he appreciated it.

"If Skyler died of poisoning, do you think Blake knew about her allergies? Because that suggests a more intimate relationship, not a one-night hook up. I mean, you don't really tell your secrets, or weaknesses, to someone you plan to never see again."

It took her a second to notice both men were staring at her. "Who said anything about poison or allergies?" Chris's tone was sharp. Very official. Molly squirmed in her seat a little, looking at Sam. There was a mixture of amusement and surprise in his gaze.

"Uh, I can't reveal my sources?" Molly smiled brightly at Chris. She really didn't want to get DeeDee in trouble. But Chris wasn't exactly denying any theories.

"Molly," Chris said, sitting straight and closing his laptop with a snap.

Sam chuckled under his breath, leaning forward to rest his forearms on his knees.

Putting on her own professional hat, Molly stiffened her spine. "I can't reveal my sources. I'm sorry. But, would you be willing to comment on the cause of death?"

"I would not be willing," Chris said immediately.

"How about persons of interest outside of Blake Findle?"

His eyebrow arched and a slight smirk tipped one corner of his lips. He was an attractive man and she genuinely liked him. He was funny—when he dropped the tough cop routine. And he was kind. He cared about Britton Bay and the people who lived there.

"Such as?" he asked.

Fine. Maybe if you share, he will, too. "Kyle Wilks?"

Chris's brows scrunched together. "The sous chef?"

Molly nodded. "Yes. He and the victim were sleeping together. She broke it off with him the night of her murder."

When Chris closed his eyes and squeezed the bridge of his nose, Molly wondered if she should have shared that information earlier. But when? She'd stopped by, she came when he asked. She was doing her job as a citizen. *Then why do you feel like you're giving him information as leverage to get some?* Because she was. But she couldn't feel guilty when finding the killer would put a lot of issues to rest for people that she lo...*Whoa. People you care about.*

Chris stood abruptly and leaned on the table pressing both hands against the scarred top. "Molly, I need you to stay out of this. I say that both as a police officer and as a friend. I appreciate any information that you share with me. You know I do, but you're putting yourself in danger if you dig for information someone doesn't want uncovered."

Feeling chastised, she looked down at her hands. Her heart swelled when Sam reached out for one and entangled his fingers with hers.

Looking back up, she met Chris's gaze. "I wasn't withholding information. It just came back to me when I asked you about the cause of death. If I stumble upon anything else, I'll tell you. I can't help that people talk to me."

Sam sat straighter, his body visibly tense. She didn't want to pit him between his friend and his girlfriend. She didn't want that strain between any of them.

"I know that," Chris said on a sigh. "And as frustrating as it is to have gossip swirl around this town like a damn tornado, I do appreciate your ability to glean bits and pieces people wouldn't share with police. Just make sure you remember only one of us has a badge."

Molly stood and Sam did the same. Though she felt like sticking her tongue out at him, she reminded herself that at almost thirty, she probably shouldn't. That didn't make the urge go away though. As if he sensed her desire to get the last word, Sam put a hand to the small of her back.

"Fun as always, Beatty," Sam said with not one trace of irritation in his voice.

"Likewise. Maybe we can hang out somewhere other than the station sometime soon."

Molly couldn't help her smile. "But it's so cozy here," she said.

They left the room, the three of them laughing. The buzz of computers resting traveled through the otherwise quiet bullpen area of the station.

"How are things with Sarah?" Molly asked as they walked to the reception area.

She liked the smile that lit up Chris's eyes. As though, just the mention of her name cleared the fatigue. "She's good. Really good. She got approved for the loan to open an art store. She'll be taking over the vacant shop on West Street. She's going to offer classes and stuff."

Sam clapped his friend on the back. "That's awesome, man. We should celebrate."

They hesitated at the counter, Chris leaning against it and Molly and Sam holding hands on the other side of it. "We should. Our treat since I'm going to rope both of you into helping her get the place ready. It's a decent price for the rent, but it needs some work. Landlord said if she does the work herself, he'll give her an added discount for the first six months."

Molly grinned, excited for her new friend and for the happiness that easily emanated from Chris's gaze. "We're happy to. That's so exciting. Maybe I can run a feature on her in the *Britton Bay Bulletin*. Small-town girl returns home ready to bring culture to Britton Bay."

Sam squeezed her fingers and looked down at her with a sweet smile.

"You always think in headlines?" Chris asked, covering a yawn.

She gave him a mock glare. "Often, yes. How about this one: Police officer works overtime to pay for extravagant dinner he offered to pay for when he mocks newspaper reporter."

Chris pushed off the counter. "It's kinda long."

Laughter burst from her chest and Sam joined in. "He's got you there, honey." He tugged at a lock of her hair and the affection in his gaze surrounded her, stealing her breath. Which was fine. If he was looking at her like that, she could go without oxygen for a moment or two.

Before they reached the double doors to leave, Chris called out once more. "Make sure you call me, you hear anything else."

"Yes, sir," she called back.

Sam shook his head. "You do keep things interesting."

She waited until they were in the car and on their way back to his place before she asked the question troubling her brain. "Do you feel like I'm putting a wedge in your friendship with Chris? I know I'm not his favorite person sometimes."

Sam gave her an easy smile and reached for her hand like he did so often. "I'm not worried about my friendship with Chris. He's just doing his job and so are you. I'm sure he's not your favorite person sometimes either."

She nodded. He wasn't wrong. "That's true."

The roads were quieter now and the air between them shimmered with contentment. Just a couple, heading home for the evening. Take out the murder, the missing bride, the police inquisitions, and they were nearly normal.

"I wouldn't mind earning that spot," Sam said, as they neared his apartment.

Molly turned her head, smiled at him. "What spot?"

"Your favorite person." He winked at her.

Oh, boy. She was surprised her grin didn't make her entire body glow, it felt so bright. "It's yours," she whispered.

His fingers tightened. "Then I guess we're even."

* * * *

They settled in, curling up together on the couch to watch Netflix and Molly had nearly fallen asleep with her head on Sam's chest when her phone buzzed. She stirred and mumbled, making him laugh and reach forward for her. Grabbing her phone from the coffee table, he passed it to her.

She opened one eye and stared at the text that had come in.

Unknown: I need to see you. Please. It's important. Can you meet me at the beach? Where I met your puppy?

Confusion woke all of Molly's senses. She shifted, sitting up. Sam glanced at the screen.

"Who's that?"

"I'm not positive, but I think it's Chantel."

Chapter Eighteen

Sam refused to let her go alone. She was slightly miffed over the way he took the choice from her. She'd insisted on driving her own Jeep and could feel his gaze from the passenger seat. Britton Bay was asleep right now, the sky full of stars and the streets empty.

"I can't believe you're pouting," Sam said. His tone was amused.

She shot him a glance that she wasn't sure he could see in the dark interior of her Jeep. "A two-year-old pouts. An independent woman approaching her thirties does not. I just don't appreciate you going all alpha and deciding I can't take care of myself."

She stopped at a stop light, her hand on the gear shifter. Sam's hand covered hers and she turned her head to look at him.

"You're one of the strongest women I've ever met. You could give lessons on being independent and capable. But as someone who cares about you, is that really what you expect of me? For me to hang out watching television in my apartment while my girlfriend goes to meet up with a stranger whose husband-to-be is in jail for suspicion of murder? You think I'd just walk you to the door, say goodnight and hope I hear from you tomorrow? I think you're mistaking the word for alpha for protective. And I won't apologize for it. Something happens to you because I gave in to your need to show you can do it alone, how am I supposed to live with that?"

Molly's mouth dropped open. The light had changed to green, but her foot was lead on the brake, absorbing Sam's words and the harsh way he spoke. "I…"

He cut her off, waving his hand and looking out onto the desolate street. "We can't always control how we feel, Molly. I'm telling myself to go slow with you because even though you'll walk headfirst into a lion's cage, you're scared of getting too close." He turned back to her now, his tone gentler. "But I would have insisted going with anyone. Jill. My mom. Bella. Cal. I'd have wanted to go even if it was Chris and he has a gun."

She swallowed both the lump in her throat and a heavy serving of guilt. "I'm sorry."

He gestured to the green light with his chin. "Light changed."

She looked back to the road and eased up on the break. "I guess I just feel a need to prove myself. I overreacted. I'm sorry."

"You said that already and I believe you. It's a two-way street, Molly. If you'd do it for me, don't even question whether I'd do the same for you."

She turned her hand so their fingers joined. The gentle squeeze he gave her both reassured her and settled her stomach. She didn't like being at odds with him and truthfully, she didn't want to go to the beach alone. Molly didn't intend to put herself in harm's way just to prove a point. *Every time he goes out of his way to show you he cares, you put your walls up.* She needed to stop doing that.

Pulling into the parking lot that was packed most days, she turned into a spot and cut the engine. There were a couple of teens embracing on the hood of a car. Their dark silhouettes pulled apart when Molly and Sam got out of the Jeep. Sam took her hand again and they strolled away from the parking lot. There was both a bike lane and a walking path that lined the ocean. The water glistened, the moon bouncing off of its dark surface and for one second, it seemed like a giant stage with the beam of light spotlighting it. Molly loved the beauty of it.

"I never get tired of that view," Sam said as they walked.

"I can see why. It's so peaceful," she agreed.

"When I finally buy a place, I'd like to make sure I can see the water," he said.

They continued to walk along the winding footpath, which curved around natural growth and bushes tended to by the city. The smell of wild sweet peas tickled her nose and she breathed it in.

"Do you think you'll do that sometime soon?"

"I'm in no rush. My apartment is fine and honestly, right now, I'm just content to pump my profits back into my shop."

She thought about that, how proud he was of what he had built with the money his father's insurance had left him. Sam's way of honoring a man he'd adored and admired. Molly wished she could have met his father, the man who left behind such a lovely wife and amazing son. She was grateful both of them suffered less now and that Katherine was seizing a chance to move forward.

"I think your dad would be very proud of you," she said, her voice lowering. It sounded so loud, even with the roll of the ocean waves in the background.

"I think so, too." His grip on her hand tightened. "We close?"

Looking ahead, seeing the path she took on her morning walks, Molly pointed. "In there, just around a curve is the stairs I use to come down."

The few trees that jutted out, like they were suspended at strange angles, shielded one area and Molly knew with absolute certainty that this was where Chantel would be. Not that she'd confirmed it was her when Molly had texted back: *Who is this?*

She wasn't scared. She didn't believe she or Sam were in any danger. Still, her shoulders tightened and her blood raced through her veins. The sound of her own breathing seemed to echo in her ears.

"Breathe," he whispered, tugging her hand.

Right. Good idea. She'd just inhaled when a rustling trapped her breath again. "Chantel?" Knowing the water made voices travel, she kept hers quiet.

"Molly?"

Who else did she expect? The woman she'd only seen a handful of times came around the bent trees and stood before them. She wore a thin sweater and a pair of jeans, her hair pulled to one side in a braid. Though it was dark, Molly didn't think she was wearing any makeup. She looked... vulnerable. And young. So different than the debutante of a woman whom she'd watched that first day.

"Who is that?" Chantel asked, her pitch increasing.

"This is my boyfriend, Sam. His mother owns the bed-and-breakfast."

Her already pale face seemed to lose another shade of color. "Did you tell anyone you were meeting me here? From the bed-and-breakfast?"

Sam smiled at her. "It's just us, Chantel. You texted Molly and I didn't want her to come here alone."

Chantel nodded, wrapping her arms around her middle. The purse she wore across her chest swung at her side when she stepped over a low-lying log and sat on it. Burying her face in her hands, Sam and Molly could only stand there, waiting. She was obviously in a serious amount of distress and neither of them knew if she'd found out about Blake yet. Molly pulled her hand from Sam's and went to sit down next to Chantel.

"What do you need?"

Chantel lifted her face, dropping her hands to her side, resting them on the log. "I need help. I need Blake out of jail because he didn't do anything and then I need to get away from my mother before I'm in jail for assault." The last part was said with a bit of humor in her tone, surprising Molly.

Molly gave her a small smile. The moon shone over them, reflecting off the water and their eyes had adjusted to the light so Molly could see the concern etched in Chantel's features. The weariness she saw in the young woman's gaze tugged at Molly's heart. She wanted to marry the man she loved. That was it; she wanted to pledge to love him forever and her wedding had literally turned into a sideshow that she had no control over.

"Why were you crying this morning?" If Molly was going to help, she needed answers.

Sam wandered a bit, close enough that she could see him, but giving them the privacy they needed to get Chantel to open up.

Chantel ran her hands up and down her jeans, like she was warming them. "He'd kind of disappeared for a bit, the first night we got here. When he came back to our room, he was agitated and I worried it was because of something my mom had done. She doesn't like him. I'm sure everyone has picked up on that." She took a large gulp of air. "I pushed and pushed and finally he snapped at me and said it had nothing to do with my mother. We argued. He said some nasty things about her that upset me. I went to the couch, but couldn't sleep. In the middle of the night, he finally came out of the bedroom—it's a really nice suite with the separate bedroom and living areas. Anyway, he obviously hadn't been sleeping either. We sat on the couch together for a while, just being together. It was quiet and calm and the most peaceful I've felt since all of the wedding plans started. Just before dawn, he said he had something to tell me."

Molly shifted, angling her body toward Chantel. So, Blake had been with her all night? Was he honest with her? She didn't say anything, even when the bride-to-be let the moment fill with silence. If she needed a minute, it was understandable.

Chantel looked out at the water. "He slept with her. The cook. He went to Vegas for a work thing a few years ago. To be fair, we'd decided to take some time apart. Not a lot of time, but we weren't actually together when it happened. But still, you know? This woman he had a one-night stand with is serving up crepes for my wedding breakfast? No thank you. So I said she had to go. I told him to fire her and I went to the beach. You came down a short while later."

It was a lot. There was a chance that she could be covering for him. Love seemed to come with a mandatory set of blinders in Molly's experience.

Laughter rang out from somewhere above them. Probably teens making the most of the final days of summer.

"How did you know he was in jail? Why did you just disappear?" More questions bubbled up Molly's throat, but she cautioned herself to slow down.

Chantel leaned over and scooped up a handful of sand, then watched it sift through her fingers, scattering down, somewhere close to where it had started. Nothing ever went back together the exact same way.

"He called. I wasn't answering, but I got his message. I was his one phone call," Chantel said. Molly wasn't sure if the woman thought that was romantic.

"I left because I couldn't take feeling torn between him and my mother, and I started to worry that my whole life would be this way and I can't constantly choose."

She shouldn't have to. "Where did you go?"

Chantel smiled, full and bright. "My aunt's. She and my mom don't talk to each other anymore. My mother couldn't wait to come back to this town and shove a big wedding in her sister's face. When I showed up on her doorstep and said I couldn't handle being around her anymore, she welcomed me with open arms."

Molly spent a lot of time wishing she'd had a bigger family. As an army brat, she always thought it'd be less of a transition moving from one place to another if she'd had a sibling or two. Getting older, she'd wondered what it would be like to have a protective older brother or a sister who stole her clothes. There were plenty of times she'd felt lonely. But it would seem, based on what she'd witnessed just this week alone, that families, large or small, were complicated things.

"Will you be going back to the bed-and-breakfast?"

Chantel shook her head. "No. I don't want to be married there. My mother wanted a big wedding there to show everyone she'd done well for herself. In truth, all she did was marry well. Since my father died, she's been trying to prove she still belongs in the same circle by doing things like this. Things for show."

She looked at Molly, her gaze sharp and intent. "But I *want* to marry Blake before I go. I don't need all of the trimmings. I thought I did, but when it comes down to whether I'd rather have all of those things or have him be my husband, it's an easy choice. Will you help me?"

Molly struggled with saying the right thing. "Chantel, you should go to the police. If you tell them what you told me, they'll know Blake has an alibi for the time Skyler was murdered."

She stood up now, slipping a little in the soft sand. "No. I can't. I know it makes me a coward, but I can't go back there. I need everyone to just leave us alone. I'm going to stay with my aunt. I'm going to marry Blake and then we're going to leave here and start our own lives. Please Molly. *Please.* If I go back, my mother will pull me in, try to convince me he's terrible for me. I know who he is. I know he has a past. Don't we all? I don't care about that. He's not hiding anything and he wouldn't hurt anyone."

Molly stood as well. She honestly didn't know what she could do to help if Chantel wasn't even willing to go to the police station for the man she said she loved. "But he has a history of assault." Those blinders again.

Chantel scoffed. "He does. His cousin pressed charges after Blake beat him badly enough to break some bones."

Pressing her lips into a firm line, Molly stared at the woman, wondering how that evidence helped Blake.

"He and his cousin were at a bar. It's a long story, but his cousin hit on a woman who didn't want his attention and took it way too far. He ended up grabbing her and shoving her. Blake intervened and he was the one that had charges laid against him. The girl didn't want to talk about it."

Why does every story have a dozen sides?

Chantel sighed, like she was out of energy. "I'll be at my aunt's. I understand if you don't want to help me. I just had to try."

"Why me?"

Chantel pursed her lips. Behind her, Sam was throwing rocks into the ocean. "You asked if I was okay. You don't even know me and you cared. You were genuinely concerned with *me*. The only other person who's been concerned, is Blake. He's made mistakes, but he loves me. And I love him."

"What if I can't do anything?"

She shrugged. "I don't know. Maybe I can leave an anonymous tip or something, saying he has an alibi. I could phone the police station, I guess. But if they ask me to come in and I don't, they may not believe me."

Molly sighed. She did care. About too many people and things. Chris didn't want her involved, but if she could connect him with Chantel in a way that didn't let everyone know where she was, he could take it from there. He wouldn't want to be holding an innocent man. *If she's telling the truth.*

"If what you said is true, someone else killed Skyler. If we can get the police onto other suspects, they'll release Blake."

"They can only hold him for forty-eight hours, but he shouldn't have to stay there at all," Chantel said. "They don't have enough to hold him longer."

Sam wandered back over, took Molly's hand. "What are they holding him on now?"

Chantel's lips tipped up at one corner. "Suspicion of his involvement, obstruction of an ongoing investigation, and refusing to cooperate and damage of property. It seems that while he was getting a ride to the motel, he didn't like being questioned by your sheriff and smacked his fist against the dash, creating a small crack. They wanted a reason. He gave them

one. Now I have to find a way to help him without letting anyone know
I'm still in town."

Molly's brain was spinning. Blake didn't seem like the sharpest knife
in any drawer, but Chantel was just a woman who'd come to get married.
It was ridiculous the way something so simple and natural had exploded
into a nightmare for her.

The other thing that had Molly caving was knowing the real killer was
still out there.

"There may be a way we can help you give your statement to the police
without alerting your mom or your bridal party."

For a second, it seemed like Chantel might hug her, but she clasped her
hands together, folding them against her chest. "Thank you."

Molly nodded. "But Chantel, you should find a way to tell them all to
go home. It isn't fair to keep everyone worrying. Your mother may have
gone overboard and she could be entirely in the wrong, but she still loves
you. So do your friends. They deserve to know you're safe."

She nodded, but said nothing as she walked toward the steps that led
up the hill to the street. Sam and Molly stared after her.

"You believe her?" he asked.

"I'm not sure. I think she's too tired to cover for him honestly. I think
if he wasn't really with her, she would have left town entirely. But she
doesn't want to go without him." She sighed.

"What now?"

Molly looked up at him. "We need to get a hold of Chris and talk to
him about Chantel, see if he'll go to her and explain why. But we should
wait until morning. I want to see if she'll tell her mom and her friends.
It'll say a lot about her if she doesn't and they're forced to just sit around
worrying and wondering. So, I need to be up early." They were closer to
the bed-and-breakfast than his home.

Sam looked down at his feet. "Want me to just drop you off at your
place since we're right here."

She smiled, turning into him and going up on tiptoes. He looked up,
his hands encircling her waist.

"Instead of dropping me off, you could just stay."

His smile moved all the way into his gaze. "You sure?"

Surer than she'd realized. "I am."

As he kissed her, he pulled her closer and Molly pushed everything else
aside. Everything other than her, him, and the sound of the waves lapping
against the shore. Maybe blinders weren't such a bad thing.

Chapter Nineteen

As it turned out, tired or not, Molly didn't head straight to bed. When they arrived at the bed-and-breakfast, they were both surprised to see the level of activity happening. Music played from a small speaker that perched atop one of the tables. Four of the groomsmen and one of the bridesmaids were playing poker. Three of the other bridesmaids were playing a board game at a table close by. All of them were chatting back and forth, both at the tables and between them. One of the other groomsmen was talking to the sous chef...what was her name again? Molly wracked her brain a second, realizing how tired she was. Shannon. Shannon Crombie. She was transferring appetizers to a smaller plate at a table that was set up under one of the tents.

And where's Mr. Kyle Wilks; sous chef and jilted lover? As if she'd conjured him, she saw him chatting up one of the blonde bridesmaids who wasn't ensconced in a game. They were sitting on the steps of the front porch, close enough so their knees were touching.

"It's kind of weird," Sam said under his breath. Not quite a whisper, but sufficiently low so he wouldn't be overheard. "Like everything is just moving forward."

"It does have a certain eerie feel to it. But what else can they do. I would imagine they can't leave until the police have okayed it."

"You're not going straight to bed, are you?" Sam looked down at her, squeezing her hand affectionately.

"I'm feeling a little chatty all of a sudden," she said, feeling her cheeks warm.

Sam chuckled, also low and under his breath and the sound sent happy shivers dancing over her skin. Lowering his head, he kissed her cheek.

"Grab some of those appetizers on your way in. I'm going to run grab Tigger and I'll be back soon."

Smiling up at him, feeling grateful, she nodded. "Deal and thank you."

She watched him take the path to his truck and wondered which approach to take. She decided to start with Shannon, who'd broken away from the table and was walking toward the back of the house, likely to enter through the kitchen. She was balancing a white pastry box in one hand and several empty plates in the other.

"Here, let me help you," Molly said, reaching for the plates.

"Oh, you don't have to," Shannon replied, but she gave up the dishes when Molly insisted.

"I'm Molly. I live in the cottage over there," she said, walking beside the petite blonde.

"Shannon. Bet you never expected this much drama from living here, huh?" She took the steps ahead of Molly and opened the door into the mud room that led to the kitchen.

"I thought it would be a happy celebration. I'm sorry about your friend or your boss…I'm sorry for your loss," she muttered, cringing at her own fumbled words.

Molly shut the door behind them and followed the cook into the kitchen. It was nowhere near as organized and neat as it had been the other night. Shannon set the box down and took the plates from Molly.

"Thanks. I'm not really sure how to define her. She was both, but not quite either, if that makes any sense. I just can't believe she's gone. It seems surreal. I keep expecting her to come through the door and rip my skin off for having the kitchen this messy," Shannon said. She leaned against the counter and brushed a few strands of hair out of her face.

There was a hint of sadness in her eyes, but something that stood out to Molly was that the woman no longer looked anxious. The slight tinge of humor in her voice suggested she didn't mean her words about Skyler yelling at her, but the relaxed set of her shoulders said the worry had been very real.

"Are you guys sticking around?"

Shannon looked at her fingernails. "No choice. Police say we can't leave. It's weird to be stuck here and not even be sure if the wedding is happening. We can't stay here indefinitely so they'd better figure out who did it quick. I'm just trying to keep everyone fed. Kyle should be helping me, but Kyle is…" she stopped and looked up. "Kyle."

If that was supposed to cement ideas in Molly's head, it didn't. "What happens if the wedding is off?" They obviously didn't know about Blake's arrest.

Shannon pushed off the counter and started straightening up the kitchen. "We go when the police say we can. There's enough food here to feed everyone for days. Police included. But now that Skyler's gone, there's no restrictions on food, so it's not like they can't bring in other food."

Molly stepped forward, under the guise of helping, but her skin tingled with awareness. "Restrictions?"

Shannon opened the dishwasher, glancing briefly at Molly. "Skyler had some allergies so only approved ingredients and foods were allowed in her kitchen."

Some allergies? "Oh. That must have been hard, being around food and not being able to taste certain things." Molly had seen enough of *Master Chef* to know that tasting your dishes mattered.

Shannon smiled, collecting the plates Molly had carried in. "Hence the restrictions. That way, she could taste everything. She didn't touch anything she didn't make."

Which meant that whoever poisoned her, knew about her allergies. "How well-known were Skyler's allergies?"

Shutting the dishwasher, the chef furrowed her brows. "It wasn't common knowledge. She kept it under wraps, but it doesn't matter now. Obviously, as her staff, we had to know."

Kyle probably knew more than most people who worked alongside her. His sadness over the breakup suggested they were more than now and again lovers. He might have hurt her, but he cared about her, too. Would she have trusted him implicitly? Skyler didn't seem like the kind of woman who trusted anyone other than herself. Or maybe someone she'd known a very long time.

"You were the sous chef in the contest Skyler won?"

It could have been Molly's imagination, the light in the room, or the fact that she was tired and wanted nothing more than to curl up with Sam, but Shannon's features stiffened. Her shoulders went just a little straighter. Her eyes widened and her mouth firmed. She pulled a cloth from one of the bins on the floor—supplies—and began wiping the counter, giving Molly her back.

"I get so tired of talking about how she won some small-town contest."

Not exactly an answer. She stared at the woman, waiting.

"We've known each other a long time. Our professional journeys began together."

Molly took that as a yes, but was still trying to decide if Shannon was choked up over the loss of her friend, or if she'd simply pushed too far, when Kyle walked in. The bridesmaid he'd been chatting with had her arm looped through his.

"Sorry about the mess, Shan. Was going to help, but got preoccupied." He glanced at Molly, gave her a once-over with his eyes that had her skin crawling. The redhead on his arm either didn't notice or mind. Kyle picked up the box Shannon had carried in and opened the top. "Mind if I take these up to her room with us?"

Molly's mouth nearly dropped open.

Shannon turned and faced him, giving the bridesmaid a once-over that, had she been paying attention, would have had her quivering. There was no softness in her gaze and it changed her features entirely.

"I suppose you're not coming back to the hotel tonight?" Shannon said.

Kyle had the nerve to wink at her. "Don't worry, love. I won't be long. Be back by the time you clean this up. Wouldn't dream of leaving you alone at Murder Motel."

Shannon cringed and the bridesmaid clued into the conversation enough to do the same. Molly felt bile rise in her throat at his crass behavior.

"You seem like you've gotten over the break-up reasonably well," Molly said, without giving her words much thought.

Kyle's fingers scrunched the white box, creating a dent. "Who are you? Wait, you were in here the other night. Upsetting Skyler."

"Molly. I live on the property. I was at the hospital after Skyler's body arrived. Saw you there." She left the words hanging in the air.

His gaze turned mean, those dark eyes narrowing and even though he didn't move, Molly felt crowded. "You know the old saying, the best way to move on from loss is to celebrate life."

Shannon made a sound of disgust. "Pretty sure that's not a saying. There is one about a snake in the grass though."

"Maybe I should wait upstairs," the bridesmaid said to Kyle.

He smiled at her, the sinister gaze disappearing like a puff of smoke. "Do that, doll. I'll be up in a minute."

He watched her go with a lecherous grin then turned back to Shannon and Molly, doing a complete Jekyll and Hyde.

"What's your problem, Shannon?" Kyle stepped closer to the petite woman and Molly wondered if he'd do anything stupid with a witness.

Shannon didn't cower. "My problem is you. We still have a job to do. I can't do it by myself and you're getting paid right along with me. You act all broken up over Skyler and then you hook up the first chance you get."

"Skyler and I were over before we began. High maintenance chicks never stick around for long. And I've done my job. There isn't even a wedding happening."

Molly didn't know how to interject to ask a question when she thought she might have to step between them to break up their argument.

"You're both upset about the loss of Skyler. Maybe everyone should call it a night and get some rest."

Both of them looked at her. "Unfortunately, I'm not okay with doing my job halfway so I can't leave the kitchen like this," Shannon said.

"It's some dishes and leftovers, Shannon, not a seven course meal. Cut the drama. I'll deal with breakfast tomorrow so you can get some sleep. Maybe it'll put you in a better mood."

Once again, they locked eyes. Molly remembered staring contests in grade school—no one wanted to break first.

"Does anyone else know about Skyler's food allergies, other than you two?" Molly had to know.

Kyle turned to her and regarded her carefully, as if he was deciding whether he could trust her. She didn't need his trust and he certainly didn't have hers. At the moment, he was racing to the top of her suspect list.

"Skyler kept that information close. We sign a nondisclosure clause. But before you go blaming anyone, lady, remember Shannon and I have nothing to gain with Skyler dead."

Molly nodded, keeping her expression neutral. The truth was, murder wasn't always about gain. In fact, it was more often about revenge. "I wasn't suggesting such a thing. There'll be a brief story in the local news tomorrow morning and I wondered if that would be something she'd want kept under wraps." Sam might be able to read her, but these two couldn't, so hopefully they'd believe what she said.

"It wasn't something she spread around," Shannon said, turning away and going back to the cleaning.

"But it must have been hard on her and on you guys," Molly pushed.

"She could take care of herself. Never touched something she didn't make on her own. Ever. There was nothing to spread around because she made sure it was never an issue." Was he defending her? She knew people grieved in different ways. The hint of pain she heard in his tone made her wonder if that's what he was doing. With the bridesmaid, the outburst... all of it. But the anger she'd seen in his eyes had been very real as well.

Kyle stared at her for a minute then, without even a glance in Molly's direction, left the room.

The quiet tension made the room feel warm. Molly turned to leave, feeling oddly dismissed. Before she got to the door, Shannon spoke in a low voice.

"I'm sorry she's gone, but I doubt she'll be missed by many."

The woman didn't even turn around to say the words. It was almost as if she'd said it to herself. Molly wondered why, if that were true, the chef sounded so forlorn when she'd said it.

* * * *

Molly woke before Sam. She took a moment to stare at his handsome features, so soft and peaceful in his sleep. His hair was an adorable mess, making her fingers itch to smooth it out. Tigger whined and she slipped out of bed to let him out. Pulling on a robe, she let him out the back door into the small fenced yard behind the cottage. Shuffling to the kitchen, she started some coffee and turned on her laptop. While it booted up, she grabbed two mugs and pulled out the muffins she'd bought. It would work for breakfast, but she really needed to do some shopping.

She poked around on the internet, looking for information on Kyle and Shannon. There was a brief bio on Shannon on the contest website, along with other members of Skyler's team. About her recipe, which she called Star Fall Macrons, Skyler was quoted saying, "Like all artists, I draw inspiration from life."

Molly scrunched her brows trying to figure out what that even meant. Kyle had a Facebook page that only confirmed Molly's thoughts of him. He was a player and judging by the number of selfies he took, an arrogant one. Under jobs, he had a long list of restaurants and when she cross-checked, there were four that matched Skyler's job history.

"Which means you've known about her allergies for a long time."

"You know you're talking to yourself, right?" Sam asked, coming into the room. He rubbed a hand over his face, blinking at her. He was cute in the morning. *He's cute all the time.* She couldn't stop her smile. Just seeing him pulled her away from the negativity swirling in her brain over the murder.

"Good morning," she said as he came closer. He crowded her, wrapping his arms around her from behind and pressing a kiss to the crown of her head.

"Morning. Did I snore or something?"

He had a little, actually, but she angled her head to give him a confused look. "What?"

He gestured to the screen with a nod of his head. "Looking for a replacement?"

Molly laughed and Sam squeezed her again before going to the cups and pouring them both coffee.

"I'm definitely not looking for anyone to replace you, as if that's even possible. *But,* if I were, it would *not* be this guy."

Jumping off her stool, she walked to the door and let Tigger in. When she came back, Sam was sipping his coffee.

"That's the sous chef, right? I still can't believe you said he hooked up with one of the bridesmaids."

"Yes. It appears his heart mends quickly."

Sam smirked at her, setting down his cup and pushing hers across the counter to her. "Hate to say it, but guys like that don't think with their hearts."

That wasn't news to Molly, but it did make her wonder. "Even if he didn't love her, he might have killed her out of anger."

Sam shrugged. "Guys like Kyle aren't usually willing to put in the energy. But maybe he wanted to teach her a lesson or something. He poisons her, but thinks it'll just make her sick?"

"Maybe." Molly went back to the computer, sliding onto the stool. "I have a bad feeling about him."

"I know. But that doesn't make him the murderer."

She couldn't disagree. "Can you call Chris and ask him about meeting with Chantel? I'm going to text her and tell her as soon as she tells her mother to call off the wedding, we'll see to it that he goes to her and takes her statement."

He broke one of the muffins in half and set it on a plate. "Sure. I have a couple of brake jobs today and some paperwork. You want to do something different tonight? Go see a movie, go swimming? Something to get your head out of all of this?"

She did. But she also knew her head would stay submerged until they caught the real killer. "Why don't we take Tigger down to that spot on the beach you showed me earlier this summer?"

Taking a large bite of the muffin and tossing a bit to Tigger, he nodded. Molly grabbed the dog food and filled the pup's bowl.

"I need to get into the paper," she said, taking the other half of the muffin.

"Text Chantel first," he said, coming to give her a kiss on the cheek before he went to get dressed.

She smiled after him and typed a quick text.

*We can get Officer Beatty to come to you first
thing, but you need to tell your mom. Everyone is
just waiting here, Chantel.*

The bubbles popped up instantly. *I sent her a text and told her I didn't
want to see or talk to her and to tell everyone to go home. I just want
Blake released.*

Molly stared at the incoming message and shook her head. She understood
the frustration and the anger, but surely, with the trouble everyone had
gone to for her wedding, she could have been mature enough to have a
conversation with her mother. Maybe it was a good thing the wedding
had come to a halt since it was more Patty's vision than Chantel's, but it
was still the bride's responsibility, in Molly's mind, to be accountable for
her behavior. She owed it to her guests to reach out to her mother and the
wedding party.

After Sam arranged for Chris to meet with Chantel, Molly and Tigger
headed to the *Britton Bay Bulletin*. Parking behind the building, where
she'd found Tigger not so long ago, she was shocked when she saw who
was waiting there for her.

Getting out of the Jeep, she lifted Tigger to the ground, hanging onto
his leash. "Mrs. Lovenly. This is a surprise."

The woman was still polished, from her perfectly coifed hair to her shiny
white heels, but the dark circles under her eyes gave her away. "I need to
know you aren't going to do an article on Blake being the murderer. I can't
have my daughter subjected to that kind of ridicule."

Molly sighed and unlocked the back door of the *Britton Bay Bulletin*.
"Come in."

The woman followed, her heels tapping against the cement and then
the hardwood entry.

"I need my photos back as well. There won't be a wedding. I told her
he was bad news."

Molly didn't have time, or the energy, to deal with this woman's drama.
She and her daughter needed lessons in communication. When Molly
unleashed Tigger, he went running through the office, most likely to find
his toys. She turned and faced Patricia and gave it to her straight.

"I'm sorry about the wedding. But I truly don't think that the reason
behind the wedding not happening is because Blake murdered Skyler."
She hoped, very much, to prove to Chris today that the most likely suspect
was Kyle. If what Chantel said proved true and Blake was released, the
officer had to at least consider her reasons, right?

"He's in jail." The disgust in her tone rivaled the contempt.

"He is. And Chantel believes he'll be released very soon. Your daughter and you don't see eye to eye about the wedding. I'm sure it's been stressful, but in the end, it's her day and she needs to make the decision. If there's anything I can print in the paper that would help you make cancelling arrangements easier, I'd be happy to."

Patricia's lips quivered. "I just want to watch her get married. I want her to be happy."

Molly studied her, trying to determine if that was true. "Then why the big fuss over the bed-and-breakfast and the fancy chef?"

Tears filled the woman's eyes, but Molly wasn't quite ready to believe they were genuine yet. "Every mother wants to give her daughter what she never had. My wedding, despite the fact that my husband came from money and earned a bucketload of it during our marriage, was plain. There was nothing special about it."

Molly couldn't understand how that could be true. "Wouldn't marrying the person you love make it special enough?"

Patricia's tears disappeared and she scoffed. "You're all so young and naïve. Love doesn't fix everything. Trust me, when the hard times hit, it's money and your place in society that are lifesavers, not love. When your husband cheats on you, it hurts a lot less if you can throw his money around like confetti. This was my chance to show my family they were wrong about me. It's me who has enough money to give my daughter everything she wants and more. Me, who doesn't have to stay here after these few awful days are over. I'm the one who made it out." She pointed at her chest, poking her finger into it.

"Do you even know what it is Chantel wants?"

Patricia didn't answer the question and that in itself was an answer. It was in Molly's nature to bridge gaps and find solutions. It was how she helped her writers pull stories together to be meaningful. So she gave Patricia something she hadn't planned on and decided the woman could do with it what she wanted.

"I can tell you. And if you really want just her happiness, you'll give her this."

Clearly frustrated with not being the one to call the shots, Patricia's lips pursed. It felt like time stopped, but eventually, with the slightest nod of her chin, she agreed. "Tell me how."

Chapter Twenty

At nine a.m., Molly okayed Jill to post the news that the police had a suspect in custody for the murder of Skyler Friessen on the *Britton Bay Bulletin*'s Twitter feed. Within ten minutes of that, a post went up on the Facebook Event page that existed for Chantel and Blake's wedding saying that 'in light of recent events' the wedding had been canceled.

At ten thirty eight a.m., Chantel texted Molly.

> *Officer Beatty came to take my statement.*
> *Hopefully it'll be enough. I don't know how to*
> *thank you.*

Molly had been crossing her fingers for exactly that text. She was so certain that Blake was the wrong suspect, she had an idea that would give Chantel the closure she needed on this entire week. Molly responded: *Can you meet me at 'our' spot tomorrow night? I'll explain after. Both of you.*

The word delivered switched to read. Molly stared at her screen, mentally crossing her fingers, then actually crossing her fingers. *Please, please.*

Chantel responded: *I guess. As long as Blake is with me.*

Confidence that he would be, rushed through her. Molly's fingers flew even as she did a mental fist pump. *Perfect. See you then.*

Jill came into Molly's office with a hard copy of the article to be printed in tomorrow's edition of the *Britton Bay Bulletin*. They'd been running extra issues all week as well as keeping up on their social media feeds. Clay didn't seem to notice that Jill had taken over that piece. He was good at layouts so Molly hoped he just accepted his limitations.

"Thoughts?" Jill sat in the chair across from her as she handed the paper to Molly. No matter how technology advanced, if Molly was editing a final draft, she needed a physical copy in her hands.

"Let's see." Molly focused on the article, which she'd assigned to Jill after they'd pieced all of the little snippets of information they had together.

Gone Too Soon
Story and Photographs by Jill Alderich

Skyler Friessen, 24, passed away this past Thursday, as mentioned in the online edition of the *Britton Bay Bulletin*. Police are still looking for information regarding the events leading up to her death, but currently have one suspect in custody. Sheriff Saron, of the Britton Bay Police Department stated: "While we truly believe this is an isolated incident, we are treating this as a homicide investigation. Anyone who was staying at the hotel at the same time as the deceased, and who has not been questioned, is asked to come by the station to give a statement. Sometimes, things you think are irrelevant are the final clue we need. We are hopeful that this case will be solved in the immediate future so we can provide closure for the family."

When asked why he doesn't believe anyone else is in danger, the sheriff responded, "The way Ms. Friessen passed leads us to believe she knew her killer, either very well or at least enough to engage in conversation privately. This was personal and targeted. Of course, if you see or hear anything that seems suspicious, we recommend calling the station and reporting it. We take care of our own here and that includes those just passing through."

Molly looked up, her eyes stinging. "It's so sad. She was so young and ready to move to the next stage."

Jill sighed. "I know. The really sad part is, I don't think she was enjoying this stage. She wasn't a happy woman."

Nodding, Molly made a few corrections and passed it back to Jill. "It's a good article. Thoughtful and kind. Has her family come into town yet?"

"Not that I've heard. I can find out?"

Molly shook her head. "No. If they're here, we should let them be. I'm hoping by the next edition, this will all be behind us."

"Think they'll release Blake?"

Molly stayed positive. "I'm sure they will. They don't have enough to charge him."

Nodding, Jill shifted gears. "I'm heading to the beach. They're doing the annual end of summer tourists versus locals beach volleyball. I'm taking the camera."

"Sounds good. I'll try to check it out later," Molly said, not really in the mood for a crowd.

"I haven't seen it in a few years. Vendors set up booths and tables with crafts and food. You and Sam should pop by tonight. There's a live band," Jill told her.

"We were thinking of going to the beach so maybe."

Molly waved goodbye, not sure why she felt so unsettled. They'd reported the news. They were doing their job. It wasn't up to her to figure out how to prove Kyle's guilt. *Or innocence.* She typed his name into her web browser again, scrolling through the few hits she found. In the main office, she heard Clay laughing and Elizabeth joining in. They were getting along better, but truthfully, Molly didn't know how long Clay would stay at the paper. Jill could cover what he did, but with Hannah going back to school full time in a week, they were already looking at adjustments to their workload.

Worry about that when it happens. The bell they kept over the front door jangled, but Molly figured it was Jill leaving for the beach.

Clay knocked on her door a minute later. She looked up from her search.

"Somebody here to see you," he said, then stepped aside.

A tall man, probably around her age, with dark gelled hair stepped through the doorway. He wore a blue polo shirt and a pair of dark pants. His posture and smile were what Molly considered "camera ready" and she labeled him as a reporter immediately.

He stepped forward, flashing his perfectly straight white teeth. "Ethan Dorsey. Reporter for the *Nevada Times*."

Molly stood, coming around the desk, and shook his hand. "Molly Owens. Editor. Welcome to Britton Bay."

She recognized the name as she'd seen it attached to many of the online articles she'd read about the competition.

"I was the feature reporter for the Mabel Bay Culinary Competition. I was shocked to hear the winner had passed away."

"You saw that on Twitter?" Molly leaned against the edge of her desk. She'd noted the increase in followers for their paper.

"I did. She's got a large following on there and Instagram. Her personality comes across less abrasive online than in person, I guess."

He'd obviously spent time with Skyler. "Do you want to sit down? I'm sure you're here to follow up, but if you're open to it, I wouldn't mind asking a few questions."

With a smile too wide for the conversation they were having, he nodded. "Of course. It's important to share information in our jobs, right?"

Molly nearly replied, "Said no reporter ever," but since she still wanted answers from him, she bit her tongue. Ethan Dorsey had an agenda. But so did she.

"Are you here to follow up on Skyler?"

He nodded, pulling out his phone and holding it up. "Just going to take some notes, if that's all right. And yes. Such as sad end to a very short career. Can you tell me about the event she was catering?"

Interesting. Molly tilted her head. "Did you stop by the bed-and-breakfast?"

His cheeks pinkened. "I did. The owner said she wasn't answering questions or giving tours of her home. That the best source of information was the police. Since that's not always the easiest route, I did a little digging and saw that you were in charge here."

"Actually, Mr. Benedict owns and runs the paper. I'm just an editor."

"Editor in chief."

She held his gaze. "What is it you want to know?"

"She had a habit of making enemies in the competition. Was never worried about making friends. She died one day into being here. No arrests made yet. I'm just wondering what happened to our hometown girl and hoped maybe you, as overseer of this fine news source, might be able to give me a few details about her final hours. You'd have considered that, right?"

Why did she feel like she was being interviewed? "It wouldn't have been very hard. She posted on her Twitter feed well into Wednesday night and we announced her death late Thursday morning."

He tapped away on his phone, looking up at her while his thumbs flew. "Sure. Sure. But we both know that what you share and what you know are two different things. I looked into you as well, Ms. Molly Owens. You've edited for some big magazines, large news outlets, and even publishers. You're trained to share the information in minimalist form."

Molly almost chuckled. "Is that what I'm trained for? Good to know. I'm not sure I can offer you much, Mr. Dorsey. You're right, Skyler didn't make friends when she got here. I tried to speak to her and she was not receptive. When I asked to interview her about her actual talent, about food and cooking, she appeared more open. Anything to do with the contest set her off."

She picked up a pen and tapped the tip of it on a notepad. "The police haven't found anything of significance."

"Small towns, huh?" He gave a conspiratorial smile that turned Molly's stomach. It was only because she wanted to ask him a few things about the competition that she didn't end the conversation.

"Our police department is doing everything they can to find her killer."

"Heard she was found by a local crazy?"

Molly gripped the pen tighter. "I'm not sure that I have any further information for you."

This man was part of the reason she hadn't enjoyed editing for larger conglomerates. Britton Bay might be small and despite recent events, very quiet, but Molly felt good about what was printed and shared online. No one at the *Britton Bay Bulletin* was looking to race up the ladder. They were where they wanted to be, which, in her opinion, removed the harsh competitive streak that could exist in some work environments.

"Where are Skyler's sous chefs?"

"Staying at the hotel until the police have okayed them to leave town."

"Pretty big damper on someone's wedding event. I stopped by the bed-and-breakfast and, before I was asked to leave, noticed they were tearing down the tents and tables."

Molly smiled. She could imagine Katherine's response to a slick talking, slick looking man who thought he could charm a story out of anyone.

"It's been very sad for everyone involved. Would it be all right if I asked you a couple of things for my own curiosity?" Molly hoped her earlier tone hadn't changed his mind about sharing.

"Why not. I'm here anyway." He didn't seem happy that he'd wasted his time, but since he could have phoned Molly for the information, she didn't feel bad.

Pressing the top of the pen, she wrote Ethan's name at the top.

"What was Skyler like during the contest?" Molly wasn't entirely certain what she was digging for, but something wasn't fitting together. Skyler's small pleasure of fame and her bad attitude just didn't seem worth killing for. Perhaps if she knew more about the woman, she could figure out what would drive someone to hurt her.

"She was intense. Hard-core, really. She almost lost a couple of times. I only tried once to talk to her during the actual competition—we could do that—circle the stage while they were in the middle of preparations and ask them questions about how they were feeling, what they were doing, what they thought of the other contestants."

"It doesn't sound as though she'd changed much. She definitely liked to be in charge of her kitchen," Molly said, not writing anything down. It was nothing she didn't know.

"She and the third-place finalist got into some pretty heated battles. She's very strict about her work area. No one who isn't approved is allowed near anything she cooks. The other guy liked getting in her space, provoking her. I'm not sure if it was for the drama of the show or what, but it came off real enough."

"Wow. I'm not sure I could handle that much drama. I didn't see any of that online. I only watched some of the last episode though."

"Oh, they ended up not showing it in the footage. They edited the material to take him out entirely because of how he was eliminated."

"What do you mean?"

"He vandalized her station, which violated the rules of the contest. They booted him, cut him from the contest and all the footage."

Sitting straighter, fingers buzzing like she'd touched a live wire, Molly tried to stay calm when she asked, "That sounds like someone with an axe to grind. Is it possible this person would want revenge?"

Ethan frowned. "Would have been nice for the added touch of drama, but no. They clearly worked things out."

Did he realize how callous it was for him to suggest more drama would have been nice for the woman who was murdered only days ago? Skyler Friessen obviously had more drama than she could handle. And it had led to her death. Maybe they'd been looking at things all wrong. Maybe someone had followed Skyler to town, lying in wait for their chance. The sheriff said it was personal. Skyler knew her attacker.

"What makes you so sure they worked things out?"

Leaning back in the chair, he crossed one foot over his knee. "I doubt she would have taken him onto her team for this latest event if they were at odds."

It didn't click at first. The words replayed in her head on a loop. Her team. Her team only included two people.

Molly slapped the pen down on paper. "What was the contestant's name?"

The reporter looked at her as if she'd just asked what her own name was. His eyebrows rose, and he leaned closer. "Kyle Wilks. Surely you know he's on her team."

He looked at her like Blake had looked at the sheriff the other day: like she was too small-town to connect the dots. But he had no idea how many dots she'd just strung together to make what was, in her mind, a very clear picture.

Chapter Twenty-One

The air in the room felt charged and heavy. Her skin felt too tight to contain the energy coursing through her.

"I actually didn't realize Mr. Wilks had been in the competition," Molly said, shocked that her voice sounded smooth and rational. Glancing at her phone, she picked it up and held it up to him. "I apologize, but I forgot I have an important meeting to get to. If you have any more questions, Elizabeth, out front, can help you."

Molly didn't wait for him to respond, even though she heard his sounds of protest. She grabbed her purse, stuck her phone in her pocket and headed for the back door. "Be back later."

No one questioned her, and she was in her Jeep within a literal minute of Dorsey telling her the news that was currently blocking her airway. She gripped her steering wheel, straightening her arms so her back pushed into the seat.

"Breathe. Breathe." After three attempts to click her seat belt into place, she finally pulled out of the *Britton Bay Bulletin*'s back lot, and headed for the police station. Using the 'Hey Siri' feature on her phone, she called Sam.

"Hey. I was just thinking of you."

"I think Kyle Wilks killed Skyler," she blurted.

"Aw, I miss you, too, cupcake."

Unbelievably, she laughed. "Okay. Sorry. Hi, Sam."

His chuckle calmed her breathing in a way nothing else did. "Hi, Molly. You were saying?"

"I really think it's him."

"You thought it was him last night."

"I know. But now I have even more reason. I'm not sure if he's back at the bed-and-breakfast, but I don't like the idea of your mom being there, even with others around. I'm going to talk to Chris right now."

"You really think they're in danger?"

Stopping at a streetlight, she forced her fingers to loosen on the steering wheel. He wasn't just going to go out and kill again.

"I don't think we should chance anything. Will you head over there?"

"Of course I will. Can you do me a favor and stay safe?"

She smiled even though he couldn't see her. "I can do that. I'll talk to you soon."

Once she parked at the station, Molly took a minute to text Chantel and ask if Blake had been released. When she didn't text back, she tucked her phone in her purse to head inside. Chris was coming down the station steps when she reached them. He lowered sunglasses over his eyes, but she knew he saw her.

"Molly."

"Chris, I have something important to tell you," she said, turning to walk beside him.

"I don't have time to talk right now." He didn't even look at her. Okay, fine, maybe she was a bit of a nuisance, but it was for a very good reason.

"Chris, this matters. You'll want to know this," she said.

He sighed—heavily—and stopped walking. "What is it about me that makes you think I can't do my own job?"

She stopped in her tracks, feeling like she'd been scalded with hot water. "I've never said anything like that. If you weren't good at your job and I didn't have the utmost respect for you, why would I bring you any information?"

Before he could answer, or she could tell him he was wasting time trying to avoid having a conversation with her by having a pointless one, another officer jogged up beside them.

"Ready to go, Boss?" the deputy Molly had seen the other night asked.

"Sure thing. Grab the cruiser," Chris said.

The deputy glanced at Molly, then nodded and did as asked.

"I have ten seconds, Molly."

Irritated, fueled with adrenaline, and swallowing down a small dose of hurt feelings, Molly stiffened her spine. "Then I'll make it quick. Kyle Wilks was a jilted contestant in the contest Skyler won, as well as a jilted lover. He was aware of her allergies and slept with her the night before she died. He's already moved onto a bridesmaid and last night I witnessed him become quite aggressive and hostile. I hope I haven't gone over my ten seconds."

She spun on her heel, even as a cruiser pulled up beside them, and started to stalk off. Chris called her name. Inhaling and exhaling sharply, she turned back.

"Did he hurt you?"

She frowned. "Who?"

Chris's eyebrows rose behind his sunglasses. "Wilks."

Because she was tired of being an underappreciated responsible citizen, she forgot to bite back her retort. "No, Officer Beatty. The only one who's managed that is you."

Whipping around before tears could fall, she hurried for her Jeep. Once inside, she kept her head down as the cruiser turned on their lights and headed, quickly, out of the parking lot.

Molly wasn't generally prone to tears, but all the emotion, activity, and lack of sleep was pushing at her every button. Swiping her eyes with the heels of her hands, then starting the car, she, too, left the lot. She thought of how Skyler had trusted Kyle and let him into her bed, into her life, and he had used what he knew about her—her weaknesses—against her. He was a monster. Hopefully he wasn't at the bed-and-breakfast with Shannon. *Shannon.* She could swing by the hotel and see if the sous chef was there. *Or call Sam and see if she's at the B and B.* If the police weren't going to take her seriously, she had to at least warn the woman, didn't she?

Since the hotel was on the way to the bed-and-breakfast, Molly swung by there. When she pulled into the lot, she understood why Chris had brushed her off. Whipping into a parking spot, Molly hurried out of the Jeep and toward the commotion by the pool. Kyle Wilks was being hauled out of the water by Chris and the deputy. Shannon was rushing up the ladder. She could hear them all talking, but couldn't make out the words until she was closer.

"Kyle Wilks, you have the right to remain silent," Chris began.

"What's going on?" Shannon said, grabbing a towel from one of the lounge chairs. A couple of people had opened the doors to their cottages and were watching.

"Ma'am, I'll need you to step back, please," the deputy said as Chris cuffed Kyle.

"But, what's going on?" Shannon's voice rose several octaves.

Chris's voice drowned hers out. "For the murder of Skyler Friessen."

Shannon whirled and launched herself at Kyle. "You son of a—"

With the reflexes of a cheetah, the deputy stopped her words and actions. "Nope. You need to back down, ma'am."

Shannon tried to look around the man restraining her by the shoulders. "He killed Skyler?"

"I didn't! This is garbage! Shannon, I didn't do this," Kyle yelled, wrestling with the handcuffs. Chris gave him a hard nudge that had him settling down and scowling over his shoulder.

Another officer showed up on the scene and began asking people to go back into their rooms. Kyle kept yelling at Shannon, telling her it wasn't him. He caught Molly's eye and the contempt she saw there was enough to flip her stomach like a bad egg.

"You! What did you do?" Kyle yelled. Chris glanced in her direction, but she couldn't see his eyes behind the shades.

The other two officers worked at getting people to go back to what they were doing, but when Molly looked over, Shannon just stood there, a towel wrapped around her shoulders. Even from a slight distance, Molly could see she was shivering. Walking toward her, Molly moved into the woman's line of sight.

"Shannon?"

The woman blinked a few times, then looked at Molly.

A harsh shiver wracked her body. Her slim figure could be glimpsed at through the towel. Her hair was slicked back from her face and she looked incredibly pale and small standing in a wet bathing suit, staring after someone she'd trusted as he was put into the back of a police cruiser.

"I can't believe he would hurt her," she said so low, Molly almost didn't hear her.

"I know. I'm sorry. Can I...do anything? Help you?"

"We'll need to ask you some questions, ma'am." Deputy—what was his name? Michael?—sidled up to them, glancing with recognition at Molly.

"I'm sure it would be fine if she put some clothes on first, right?" Molly said, hoping Shannon was in the right frame of mind to answer the officer.

She nodded, absently, looking at Molly. "Yes. I need to get dressed."

"Of course, ma'am. We'll let you do that, then we have a few questions to ask," the officer said, standing back and giving them what he probably figured amounted to privacy.

"Do you need anything? Can I call anyone?" Molly asked, feeling helpless.

Shannon shook her head. "No. I...I don't know. I should grab my clothes," she said, turning. Her towel fell, like she couldn't hold onto it and move at the same time. Molly grabbed it up from the concrete and settled it back on her shoulders, her fingers brushing over the woman's skin, along a tattooed line of black stars with tails that made them look as if they were shooting across the sky. Or, her shoulder, in this case.

"Here," Molly said, grateful when Shannon scooped up her clothes in one arm and gripped the towel around her shoulders with her other hand.

In her bare feet, she started to walk away, but turned back to Molly. "I...I don't know how long this will take. Can you get a message to the bed-and-breakfast? I think everyone is heading home anyway, but we were paid to do a job and I don't want them to think I'm not finishing it."

Molly's heart ached for this woman who'd lost two friends in the span of a few days. Cruelly. Bobbing her head up and down, working to keep her emotions at bay, she said she would.

"If you need anything, please let me know. Will you be by the bed-and-breakfast later?"

"Yes. If the wedding is off and I'm free to go, there's no reason to stay."

What a terrible way for all of this to end. "Please stop by to say goodbye."

A wistful smile touched Shannon's lips. "I will. Thank you for being so kind."

As the woman walked away and Molly looked over at the two officers talking, keeping their eyes on Shannon, she thought the world could use a little more kindness. And even though a killer had been caught, she went back to her Jeep feeling incredibly sad.

Chapter Twenty-Two

Molly typed up the article for the online edition of the *Britton Bay Bulletin*, sharing only the surface information about Kyle's arrest. Since she had the bulk of the information, it seemed easier than asking Jill to do it. Besides, she hoped the words would take the heaviness from her shoulders. The sadness in Shannon's eyes wouldn't leave her and she carried it around for most of the day.

Elizabeth and Alan had left the office early to celebrate Alan's wife's birthday. Clay had hung around for a bit, sullen as usual, but Molly wasn't sorry when everyone left, and she was on her own. She didn't know how to sort through the sadness of everything. And while pursuing tips and clues, she hadn't let herself absorb how horrifying the events of the last few days had been.

A woman had died. Her lover and friend had intentionally taken her life because of what? Molly knew there was a lot of bad things in the world, but it troubled her how much of it could not be made sense of.

Her phone rang, seeming to echo in the quiet of the empty building. In her office, she couldn't even hear the hum of the fridge. Tigger lifted his head from his curled position on the doggy bed on the floor. She swiped the screen, seeing it was her mom.

"Hey. How are you?" Molly shut down her laptop.

"I'm good. I'd ask how you are, but I keep seeing all the twits about what's going on where you live. How is it you move to a small town and there's more trouble there than in Los Angeles?"

Molly's laughter bubbled up. "Twits?"

"Yes. On the internet."

She shook her head, grateful that with all the bad in the world, she had her own pocket of good. "Why are you on Twitter, Mom?"

"So I can follow you."

Pushing away from her desk, Molly wandered out into the main area, shutting the window blinds as she went. "You should come see me instead."

"I need to see you. I need to see with my own eyes that you're doing okay," her mom said.

"I'm fine, Mom."

"Fine never means fine, honey. I know how you carry things. How you think you've let them go, but they drag you down. Tell me how you're really doing."

A sharp ache settled under her rib cage. Checking the lock on the front door, she decided it was time to head home.

"Molly." The mom undertone rang heavy even through the phone.

"I just don't know how anyone is supposed to know what's real and what isn't. You think you can trust someone and they stab you in the back. You fall in love and your heart gets handed to you in crumpled pieces. How do you ever really know who anyone is, Mom?"

She didn't really expect an answer as she walked back to her office and grabbed her purse, snapping at Tigger to get his attention.

"You know who you are, honey. That's all that matters. You be true to yourself without letting the world strip away your belief in right and wrong, good and bad. You be kind and fair, like you've always been. You'll end up in the right place, sweetie."

"How can you be so sure?" Tigger stretched, really getting into it and added a yawn for good measure. Tonight was a curl up with her pup and her boyfriend sort of night. A push the world and all that's wrong with it away kind of night.

"You can't be sure, Molly. You just trust your gut. It led you to where you are, and I know things are messy right now with all that's going on, but underneath, you're happy, right?"

She smiled at Tigger when he pranced over to her and flopped on her feet. She thought of Sam, his beautiful eyes watching her like she was the only thing he could see. She could hear Katherine's laugh in her mind and taste Bella's scones on her tongue. If she closed her eyes, she could picture the ocean that was right outside the door and the sweet little shops and all their quirky owners that lined the streets to it.

"Yes. I'm happy."

"Well, be safe, too, and then we'll both be happy."

"I love you, Mom."

"I love you more."

It was an ongoing, never-ending back and forth that neither of them would concede.

"That's what you think," Molly said.

She hung up and decided that her Jeep would be fine at the *Britton Bay Bulletin* overnight. "We need some fresh air, don't we, buddy?" Tigger wagged his tail in agreement.

Letting herself out the back door, she made sure it was locked and double checked her Jeep as well before rounding the building to head down Main Street. There was a park just up from the *Britton Bay Bulletin* office, which sat at the end of Main Street where it met Mercer Avenue. The road carried on, into a quiet area of small bungalows and duplexes. Park may have been a generous word for the grassy area that had an old swing set and a couple of benches. Tigger tugged at his leash, eager to head toward the expanse of green that would have endless scents for him to bury his nose in.

She laughed, noticing a couple sitting on one of the benches, but not really *seeing* them. Crossing the street, intending to let Tigger explore a little, she watched the couple get up, hand in hand, and squinting her eyes against the sun, stopped in her tracks when she recognized them.

"Hey, Molly," Chantel said, almost shyly.

Blake gave a half-grimace, half-smile and put up a hand, as if to wave. Or stop her from coming closer? He was an odd man and though she was glad he'd obviously been released, she wasn't altogether certain she liked him.

"Hi. What are you guys doing here?" She met them at the edge of the grass. Tigger continued to tug, but then seemed content sniffing Blake's shoe.

"We wanted to say thank you for your help," Chantel said.

"Yeah. Not sure if giving her statement over the phone would have had the same effect as you getting that cop to go see her," Blake agreed. Molly noted the trace of humility in his voice. Good, maybe he'd be more careful to not shoot his mouth off in the future.

"You guys will still meet me tomorrow night, right?" Molly looked at them, nerves welling up in her stomach as she thought about how many lines she might be crossing.

"You sure you can't just talk to us now? We want to get out of this town. We're still getting married. We haven't figured it all out yet, but I can't do it like I'm some sort of side show my mom needs to put on." Chantel's voice still belayed her anger, but there was more fatigue in it now.

"I really need it to be tomorrow. There's a lot going on right now and I need to get home. I want to see if Katherine needs any help with the bed-and-breakfast."

Chantel's cheeks turned rosy and she put her head down. Blake put an arm around her and squeezed her shoulder.

"We did send a message to her mom to say we were sorry for just bailing like that. Not that I had a huge amount of choice, but we do feel bad for leaving things like we did," Blake said.

Molly looked at them, the way their bodies aligned and the way he sheltered Chantel from her own guilt. Who knew why one person fell in love with another and why some relationships worked out and others fell through the cracks. She might not understand their pairing and Chantel's mother might not approve it, but Molly felt the love they shared for each other. They couldn't know what would happen in the future, but right here, right now, they were it for each other and maybe that had to be enough.

"I'm sure she'll see that in time. I have to go. Tomorrow. Our spot, okay?" Molly gave Chantel a smile and hoped some of her excitement shone through.

The curious look in Chantel's gaze suggested it did.

She waved and gave Tigger's leash a tug before she was tempted to tell them what she was up to. Walking down Main Street, she let herself focus on Chantel and Blake finding their happiness together. It didn't always work out the way it was expected to, but that didn't mean it hadn't ended up okay. When she strolled past Sam's shop, the bays were closed, and she checked her phone, realizing they hadn't touched base much today. Now that she thought of him, she missed him—the way his smile was enough to pull her out of a mood, the way he embraced Tigger, every time, like he was just as enamored with the pup as the dog was with him.

Since she was only about ten minutes from the bed-and-breakfast, she decided she'd wait to phone him. She'd see him tonight. They could hang out together without all the questions in her mind keeping them both company. When she reached the bed-and-breakfast and saw Sam helping someone load the final oversized canopy into a truck, her heart took a hard tumble. Her heart liked the feeling of coming home to him. Of finding him there. Oh, boy. She was in big trouble.

As she walked closer, she thought about Chantel and Blake again and wondered, if there was a side of Blake that only Chantel saw, that made some of the things he did and said forgivable. It would be hard to imagine the tide turning on her affection for Sam, so maybe she shouldn't have judged the couple so harshly. Sam turned and saw her and the smile on his face matched the one inside of her.

"I just walked past the shop and was thinking about you," she said as he came near. The grounds were back to normal and it seemed eerily quiet.

Sam stopped in front of her, glancing down at Tigger who went up on his hind legs to get a greeting. "Her first, bud." Then he looked at Molly, cupped her face with his hands, tipping her chin up with just the slightest pressure from his thumbs, and kissed her like they hadn't seen each other this morning. Molly let herself fall into the kiss, her free hand going to one of his wrists.

When he pulled back, coherent thoughts had left her head. "Hi," she whispered.

"Hi," he said, a slight smirk on his lips. "Okay, your turn." He crouched down and rubbed Tigger vigorously, causing the pup to become more excited and tangle himself up in his leash. Molly released it, laughing. Sam glanced up at her.

"I have a surprise for you," he said.

"I like surprises," she replied.

He stood, grabbing Tigger's leash and her hand, leading her toward her cottage. "Your mom okay?"

Sam glanced back at the house and nodded. "Yeah. She's happy it's quiet. The mother of the bride is still here."

Molly glanced up at him, a smile on her lips. "Oh. Hmm."

Sam chuckled. "Uh-huh."

When they reached her front door, he spun her toward him, pulling her up tight against his body. "There's something about you, Molly Owens."

Going up on tiptoes, she wrapped her arms around his neck while Tigger whined and ran around the grass. "What's that?"

Sam pressed a kiss to her forehead, then the tip of her nose, and finally her mouth. "I'm not sure, but it's different and special and I like it. A lot."

She started to say the feeling was more than mutual—in fact, she was worried her side was weighed down by a lot more like than he even knew—but Tigger started to bark as tires crunched over the gravel.

Sam glanced over his shoulder and Molly did the same. Her stomach tensed when she saw the cruiser.

Looking down at her with a wry smile, Sam squeezed her and stepped back. "What'd you do?"

She poked him in the ribs as Chris got out of the car, dressed in regular, everyday clothes. "Very funny."

His face was tight when he approached them. Molly was glad the door was at her back.

"Hey. You still own a pair of jeans? I thought you'd traded them all in for those nice police pants," Sam said, holding onto Molly's hand.

"You just get funnier," Chris said dryly. He glanced at Molly. "Molly. You talking to me?"

Sam looked between them and his hand tightened on hers. A show of quiet strength and solidarity. If he'd scattered rose petals at her feet, it wouldn't have been more romantic. He had no idea what she'd said or done, and Chris had been his friend for many years, but that one gesture made it clear where his loyalty lay.

"Can I come in?" Chris asked when she didn't answer. Letting them all in, Tigger included, she slipped off her shoes and took her time letting the pup out back. When she came back into the living area from the tiny hallway that led to the laundry and backyard, Chris and Sam were sitting down, chatting.

Chris sat in the chair that matched the three-seater couch that had come with the cottage. Molly sat beside Sam, their thighs touching. His arm went around her immediately and Chris leaned forward in the chair, clasping his hands between his widespread knees.

"I owe you an apology," he said.

Sam's body tensed. "Am I going to have to beat you up?"

Chris looked up and laughed. "You could try."

Molly was glad they broke the tension. She put her hand on Sam's leg. "Stop it. I'd say I owe you an apology back."

After a beat of silence, Chris gestured to Molly. "You're not going to say anything to her?"

Sam laughed and looked at her. "Do you want me to beat him up, honey?"

Happiness warmed her, and she shook her head even as she laughed. "I don't think so."

"Couldn't if you tried," Chris muttered.

Molly ignored him. "We had a disagreement today."

"Something tells me it'll be one of many," Chris replied. "I'm sorry I was so short with you and I'm guessing you understand why now, but it was never my intention to hurt your feelings or make you feel bad."

The tension returned to Sam's frame. "Maybe you two should give me a clue as to what's going on."

Molly explained the events of that morning, telling Chris everything she'd wanted to tell him after meeting with Dorsey, and as she told Sam how she'd caught him on his way to arrest Kyle.

"I shouldn't have made you feel bad. I didn't intend to. But the way he pointed and yelled at you, Molly...you've got to know that digging around could get you into some serious trouble. I don't want to see you hurt," Chris explained.

"I'll second that," Sam said quietly, looking at her. He looked back at Chris. "So, this is over now?"

"We're still building the case, but the evidence against him is stacking up. We have his prints on the to-go cup beside Skyler's bed which was half drunk. Our guess is he doctored it while she wasn't looking and left before the poison hit her system. Knowing that he was both a disgruntled lover and competitor just seals it all into place."

Something clattered around in Molly's mind. The to-go cup from Bella's. The reason Bella had been suspected.

"Why the heck would he kill her?" Sam asked, then shook his head and sighed. "Why would anyone kill? That's a better question. I'm glad you caught him, but it's too bad the wedding was so deeply impacted by this and that a woman died over such trivial things. A contest? Lives ruined over something that won't matter six months from now."

He was right, and his brain was traveling the same road hers had wandered this morning and for most of the day.

"None of that is to be printed in the paper by the way. I'd appreciate it if you kept the details quiet," Chris added.

"I think this story is one we're happy to move on from," Molly said, something still nagging at her subconscious.

"I would like to get your statement on everything Dorsey said though. Mind coming down to the station tomorrow and filling it out?"

"Maybe they should get you a desk. For when you visit," Sam said.

Molly rolled her eyes. "Ha, ha. He's right, you are funny."

Chris smacked both hands against his thighs. "Well, I'm going to get going. See if maybe Sarah is up for a movie. Wouldn't mind a distraction from all of this."

"We should catch one together soon," Sam said as he and Molly got off the couch.

"Sounds good. Maybe after this we'll go back to being a sleepy, little, nowhere town," Chris said. They walked him to the door and said goodnight. Molly noticed the sky had grown darker. On the back porch of the bed-and-breakfast, Patricia sat, a mug in hand, staring at the sky. There was a sense of loneliness in her posture that tugged at Molly's emotions. With the case closed, hopefully, tomorrow, some hearts could start to heal.

Chapter Twenty-Three

Waking up beside Sam brought a smile to Molly's face. She hadn't even opened her eyes yet, but feeling him there beside her, his arm holding her close as he slept on and dawn broke through the blinds, made her eager to start her day. Until today, they'd been using Sundays to hang around and explore each other's hobbies. Sam had taken her to a baseball game and she'd had him try paddle boarding. They'd gone bowling and decided neither of them liked it all that much. For weeks now, their Sundays had been spent wrapped up in each other and that was exactly how she wanted to spend this one.

But there were things to be done. Slipping out of the bed, she patted her leg so Tigger would follow her. After letting him out, she started the coffee, let him in, and took a quick shower. Sam was still sleeping when she started on her first cup. He came in when she was halfway through, rumpled and adorable, running a hand over his bare chest.

"Hey," he said, his voice morning rough.

"Hey, yourself."

"Why are we up so early?" He took the cup she'd just set down, while Molly swallowed the rest of her coffee before refilling her cup.

"*We* aren't. It's not that early now. I was up early because I'm excited about today. I have to go give a statement like Chris asked, but on the way, I'll tell you my plans."

"I knew you were up to something. It's why the bride's mom stayed, isn't it?"

He kissed the top of her head and she gave herself a minute to absorb his warmth and lean into him.

"Maybe."

"Guess I'd better get dressed then. You have anything for breakfast?"

"I do," Molly said, grinning at him. "We just have to stop at Bella's and pick it up."

Sam laughed, clearly more awake. "Good thing you're cute."

Back at you, she thought as he walked away. Molly checked her social media and the *Britton Bay Bulletin*'s website and email while she waited. Tigger wasn't happy about being left behind, but they could take him to the beach with them later.

Parking in front of Bella's, she met Sam around the hood of his truck, slipping her hand into his. They were almost to the door when Corky burst out of it. He was shaking his head, pulling at his matted beard. He wore long board shorts and a misbuttoned shirt. He carried a backpack on one arm.

"Hey, Corky. You okay, bud? Let us buy you a coffee," Sam said.

Corky looked at him, looked at Molly, his eyes wide and...scared. "No. No. No more coffee. I don't like the stars. I watched them go."

"Okay. Well, how about something to eat?" Sam tried to put a hand on Corky's shoulder.

"Not hungry. Have to go. I want to go." He looked back at Bella's. "I'll go to Calliope's. Calliope is nice. She's my friend."

Molly's heart hurt at the tone in Corky's voice. "We're your friends, too, Corky."

His eyes lost a little of their wildness for a brief second when he looked at her. "You're nice. Like Calliope."

Before either of them could say anything, Corky wandered off, down the sidewalk in the direction of the Come 'n Get It Eatery that Calliope owned with her husband Dean.

"I'm just going to send Calli a text, let her know he's on his way," Sam said. Molly nodded and waited beside him as he texted. She was reminded again of how Sheriff Saron had said they watch out for their own.

Sam stared after Corky, a troubled look on his face. Giving Molly a tight smile, he held the door to the bakery open for her. Inside was busy for a Sunday morning when the bulk of tourists had left. A few couples sat in booths and a couple of people sat at the long countertop that attached to one wall. Behind the counter, Bella was ringing up an order and one of her staff was making a coffee drink.

Shannon sat on one of the stools at the bar-style countertop, typing something on her phone, a coffee in her hand. Molly wanted to reach out to her—even with others around, she seemed so alone.

"Hey, guys, how's it going?" Bella asked as the customer she'd been helping left and made room for them to approach the front.

"Good, Bella. How are you?" Sam asked.

"I'm good. Starting to feel normal again." She made eye contact with Molly. "That summer cold really threw me."

Molly smiled. "I'm glad you're feeling better."

"Me, too. How about some scones on the house?" Bella moved toward the display case.

Sam laughed and looked at Molly. "Looks like she knows you pretty well."

"I'm okay with being an open book. Especially if there are scones in the picture." Turning back to see if Shannon had looked up from her phone, Molly took the chance to say hi.

Dark circles rimmed the woman's eyes. "Hey, Molly."

"Hi, Shannon. How are you?" Molly leaned against the counter but didn't take a seat.

"I'm okay. I have to give a statement today, but after that, I'm free to go."

"I bet you're looking forward to heading home," Molly said.

"I am. This is one job I'll never forget," Shannon said sadly. She set her coffee down.

Molly glanced at Sam who was chatting with Bella as she boxed up scones. "I bet. What will you do now?"

Even though she shrugged, she answered. "I need to grab a couple of things we left at the bed-and-breakfast, including the wedding cake. Kyle didn't box up all of our supplies the other day, so I'll do that."

Katherine was busy putting together the final touches on what Molly had asked for her help with. Hopefully, Patricia was with her. But she hadn't thought of a cake. She bit her lip, gnawed at it really, while more thoughts swirled.

Sam joined her and said hello to Shannon. He set Molly's coffee down on the counter, the box of scones beside it, and held onto his own. Molly debated for only a second. Her plan was all unfolding today, so she took a deep breath and then, in a low voice, told both of them what she was up to.

"Blake and Chantel are meeting me at the beach in a few hours. Your mom and Patricia are setting it up. The minister was coming today anyway. They'll be married at sunset on the beach. But I'm thinking, maybe that cake doesn't have to go to waste," Molly said.

Sam looked at her with so much affection it stopped her breath. "You organized that for them?"

"That's really nice. I'm glad they're still going to get married. And of course, the cake should be eaten," Shannon said. "No sense in it getting thrown out."

"There's never a good reason to throw out cake," Molly said.

Shoulders shaking with laughter, Sam pulled her closer. "You're a good person, honey."

Molly leaned into him, noting the sad look in Shannon's eyes. "Do you want to come to the wedding? There are a few guests who are still coming just for the evening. Patricia and Katherine contacted everyone, mostly to cancel, but there were a few people Patricia thought Chantel would want there."

Shannon nodded. "That would be lovely. I need to swing by the police station and head to the hotel to grab my stuff. After that, I'll go to the bed-and-breakfast, grab our things and the cake, and then meet you there?"

Molly shifted things around mentally in her head. "Okay, but I have to make a statement, too. An Ethan Dorsey came to see me yesterday about the contest and Skyler, and shared some information about Kyle. I have to share that on record," Molly explained. Chris had told her not to say anything, but Shannon would know who Dorsey was, so it didn't seem wrong.

Shannon's eyes widened. "Ethan was here?"

Molly nodded. "Yes. You remember him from the contest?"

Mouth drawn tight, the sous chef nodded. "He was the final judge."

That was news, though Molly didn't see how it was relevant. "Oh."

Unsure where the tension had sprung from, Molly looked at Sam who just drew his shoulders up, letting them drop just as quick

"Why don't you and I go to the station and your hotel together? Sam, we can meet you at the bed-and-breakfast and you can help transport the cake?"

"Do you want me to come with you?" Sam asked.

Molly picked up her coffee to take a sip, but Shannon grabbed at her hand. "That's mine!"

Startled, Molly knocked her coffee onto the floor and sent the bag of scones flying.

Shannon jumped off the stool. "I'm sorry. I'm so sorry. I'm so used to making sure Skyler doesn't accidentally pick up what I'm eating or drinking. We weren't supposed to have any unapproved ingredients in her kitchen, but I sneak stuff into my own food and drinks and just never told her. I'm sorry. It was instinct."

The whole time she rambled, she attempted to mop of the coffee while Molly grabbed the scones. Sam got a mop from Bella who came over with a cloth.

"It's just a spill, hon, no big deal," Bella said.

They righted the floor and the counter. Bella replaced the scones. But Shannon still stood, her face ashen. That there would be that much tension in every cell of her body, shocked Molly. *How horrible it must have been to work in those conditions, fearing you could cause harm or death to the person you work with. Unless you just follow the orders and don't bring in anything harmful.* Shannon rubbed up and down her arms, not really looking at any of them. *She didn't touch anything she didn't make.*

"You going with her, Molly? Might be best, she seems pretty shaken," Bella asked as Shannon headed for the door.

Molly startled. Shannon had said something about Skyler not touching anything that she hadn't prepared. Shannon was almost to the door and she felt like she was tripping over her thoughts.

"I'll meet you at the bed-and-breakfast?" Molly looked up at Sam. He looked concerned but nodded.

"Keep your phone on, okay? You sure you don't want me to come?"

"No, text your mom, see if she needs anything and then head over for the cake. Being ready early is better than late."

Molly kissed his cheek and hurried after Shannon, who'd obviously rented a vehicle that she was now climbing into. Going to the passenger side, she called the chef's name.

"Can I still come with you?"

Shannon blinked. "Yeah, sure."

They got in the car and Molly couldn't shake the muddled thoughts trying to sort themselves in her head. Shannon dug through her purse, found some keys and pulled them out only to drop them on the floor. Why was she so jumpy? What had gotten into her?

Don't be so callous, Molly. This woman lost two friends in the most horrible way.

"Sorry," Shannon muttered, leaning down to grab the keys. Reaching forward, her sleeve came off of her shoulder, just a little, exposing just a hint of her tattoo. Just a few points of a dark star.

And as Molly's thoughts collided into place, slamming into each other with a startling clarity, Shannon started the car and reversed out of the spot.

Throat dry, Molly told herself to breathe and think through things rationally. The killer was in jail. He'd poisoned her. *I don't like the stars.* Both times Corky had said that, Shannon had been in the vicinity. *Stop it. She was poisoned with the drink from Bella's.* Even as she made herself think the words, she knew she was lying to herself. Skyler Friessen was a woman who got what she wanted no matter the cost. If she lived by a set of rules, Molly was certain, she wouldn't flex them for anyone. Which meant that the only person who might have drunk Bella's coffee was Kyle. And since he wasn't dead, that wasn't the source of the poison. Sitting ramrod straight, fingers clutching her purse, Molly wracked her brain trying to think of that morning. The details. What had Corky seen?

The car sped up like the pace of Molly's heart. Without warning, Shannon swerved to the right with such a sharp yank on the wheel that Molly's head hit the window. Hard. Wincing and giving a howl of pain, she didn't have a chance of stopping the woman from yanking the purse out of her lap and tossing it into the back seat, well out of Molly's reach.

Head spinning, she pressed her fingers to her temple and felt warm liquid touch her skin. She was bleeding.

Aiming for ignorance, she asked, "What's going on?"

Shannon gave a harsh, abrasive laugh. "You can't hide a thing. You put it all together and it was like a neon sign went on over your head. I wouldn't suggest you play poker."

"Shannon, please." Molly didn't know what she was asking for at that particular moment.

"Couldn't just let it go. Any of you. Goddamn Ethan Dorsey was the one who wrecked everything in the first place," Shannon said, her foot seeming to stomp onto the accelerator.

"Shannon, please, stop the car," Molly said. She braced herself against the door, looking around to see if there was anything with which she could attack the woman. Nothing. Could she open the door and jump out? *Only if you want to die. Which you might anyway.* She glanced out the window, turning back to the driver when Shannon laughed loudly.

"Do it. Jump. Make it easier, please."

Molly thought of just grabbing the steering wheel and fighting the woman for control, but there were people on the streets, walking and driving and she felt dizzy enough she couldn't be sure she would avoid hitting them.

"Why?" she asked instead. Shannon couldn't drive forever.

"It was my recipe," Shannon said simply.

What recipe? What was she talking about? *Why do you keep trying to rationalize the actions of people who are not all there?*

"She didn't drink the coffee," Molly said, still not understanding how to piece things together. "Kyle said she never touched what she didn't create, which means that you doctored something she trusted. Something she wouldn't suspect."

"It wasn't supposed to kill her. Is that what you want to hear?"

"What I want is for you to slow down, preferably pull over." They were leaving Main Street behind, heading up into the residential neighborhood at a speed that had people whipping their necks in the direction of the vehicle.

"She was supposed to get sick. That's it. Just so I could take over the wedding preparations. She owed me. She stole my recipe, won the contest. She took *my* prize money to put a down payment on a spot for her restaurant. Dorsey was crazy about her. He didn't even ask about me, did he? I tried to tell him she stole my recipe. I told her it would come back to bite her. But she wasn't supposed to die."

The sound of sirens behind them both startled and relieved Molly, but only for a second. Shannon increased her speed, her grip on the steering wheel alarmingly tight.

"You can say that, you can say it was an accident," Molly said, working hard to keep her voice even. Her pulse beat such a fast, hard rhythm, she wondered how she could talk over it.

Shannon looked at her, taking a turn without even watching where she was driving. Turning her gaze back to the road and pulling on the wheel so she didn't fly into a parked car, Shannon laughed. It wasn't a funny sound.

"Right. They'll believe that." Her hands shook, making her driving more erratic.

"There's nowhere to go," Molly said, not sure if she was telling Shannon or herself.

The road continued to climb and her heart shuddered as they passed the house where Molly had found Vernon's body. A FOR SALE sign sat crookedly in the front of the overgrown lawn. Shannon started mumbling about something Molly couldn't understand but her thoughts were still on the grass. It had continued to grow because that's how life worked. It went on even when some didn't. Day after day, no matter how minute the progress, people, life—it all carried forward. That thought was both humbling and terrifying. Because Molly wanted to carry forward. She wanted to embrace the fear she felt about caring so deeply for Sam. She wanted to see her parents. And Tori. She wanted more. She wanted more days and minutes and chances to mess up and set it right.

Up ahead to the left—where the houses thinned out, the yards turned to gravel, and some new developments were starting—was a parking lot. Tourists and locals parked there to head up into the hiking trails, another pull of the Oregon beachside town.

The sirens wailed. When Molly turned, she saw two cars chasing after them and behind that, trailing in the distance was Sam's truck. Molly leaned to the side and with all of her strength, grabbed the steering wheel, hoping the surprise would give her an advantage. She pushed to the left and the car jolted in that direction. Shannon screamed and released the wheel with one hand to push at Molly's face. Her nails scraped across Molly's cheek, but Molly didn't let go. She forced the wheel to the left, seeing that she was steering them both toward a low embankment in the uneven gravel parking area. The problem—one of the most pressing ones anyway—was that Shannon kept her foot on the gas. They were inertia—and Molly needed something to stop them. Shannon gripped the wheel again, trying to turn it from the direction Molly was steering them. The car slammed over the embankment, a drop of maybe one foot that put them on an uneven, overgrown area hedged by towering Douglas firs. Molly bit her tongue and Shannon hurled curse words like rocks.

And then they stopped with a jolt that rocked Molly's arm in its socket. She smashed her elbow against the dashboard and Shannon's head shot forward, smacking into the steering wheel. The horn went off, the sirens continued to wail, and Molly felt the crushing need to close her eyes for just one minute. Shannon fumbled with her seat belt and Molly wanted to stop her, but everything hurt and even with the banging whir in her head, she knew, she wasn't alone. The doors flung open in unison, Molly heard Chris's voice barking orders. Shannon was hauled from the vehicle.

"Ma'am? Can you hear me?" the officer whose name Molly could just not remember asked, touching her shoulder.

"Molly!" Sam's voice echoed in her head and the fear, the pain intricately laced into her name sorted the jumble of her thoughts.

"Can you move?" the officer asked.

"Molly." He was closer now. She turned her head and saw him hovering over the officer's shoulder.

"You need to move back, Sam," another officer behind the kneeling one said.

"I'm okay," Molly said. She moved to undo her seat belt and winced in pain. She couldn't bend her arm. Using the other one, she clicked the release and turned her body, putting both feet outside of the vehicle. "I can stand. I'm okay."

"Let me help you," the officer said, taking her arm and causing her to cry out.

"I'll help her," Sam barked, pushing his way between them.

He leaned in, noted the way Molly was favoring her elbow and turned her so the other side of her body was leaning into him and then he lifted her, like she weighed nothing and, with the utmost care, crushed her to his chest.

"You're okay. You're okay. Tell me you're okay." His words were muffled by her hair. He'd buried his face in it and Molly let herself burrow into the crook of his neck.

"I'm okay," she whispered. She hurt, but she was okay.

"Sam, the ambulance is on its way," Chris said.

Molly lifted her head and saw that behind Chris, Shannon was being put into a cruiser, her hands cuffed in front of her.

"She's bleeding, Sam," Chris said.

Sam's body turned to concrete as he held her and she wished she could move her injured arm to run her hand over his chest and soothe him.

"I'm okay. My head hit the window. I'm okay."

Sam looked into her eyes and Molly felt like he could see all the way through her. Holding her gaze, he finally nodded. "You still need to go to the hospital."

As if on cue, the ambulance pulled into the gravel lot that was overflowing with activity. Molly rested her head against Sam's chest as he walked her toward the back of the ambulance. Two police cruisers sat, front doors open, four police officers milled about, one standing by the back of the car that held Shannon, his hand on the roof.

"What do we got?" A female paramedic pulled open the ambulance doors and Sam set Molly on the edge of the opening.

"Something is wrong with her arm," Sam said, panic still tainting his words.

"I hit it on the dashboard," Molly said, wincing when the woman touched her.

"Let's clean up the cut on your head and then we'll bring you in to the hospital for x-rays," she said.

Molly's heart lodged in her chest and Sam came closer. "What is it?"

"I don't want to go in the ambulance."

"Can I drive her?" Sam asked. No questions asked; he just took her back.

The ambulance driver looked back and forth between them, a slight smile on her lips.

"Let me just do an initial check, write a few things down, and yes, then that should be fine. We'll follow you there."

Stepping around Molly, the woman went into the ambulance, presumably to grab something to clean up Molly's scrapes and cuts.

Sam crowded her leaning in. "You scared me. I don't think I've ever been that scared." His fingers gripped hers.

"I'm okay. I promise."

The female paramedic came back with gauze, a salve, and Band-Aids. A male paramedic walked up to them.

"Other woman's injuries are superficial. They need to process her at the station, but I told them we'd check on her again later."

"Want to get her loaded and I'll drive?" he asked.

The female looked up from bandaging Molly's head. "We'll follow her."

The man frowned. "That's not typical protocol."

Sam's smile was tight and tension radiated from his body. "This isn't typical. Go figure, she doesn't trust someone else to drive her."

His gaze captured hers, swallowed her whole and alleviated the ache in every inch of her body because he knew, she trusted him.

Chapter Twenty-Four

Sam didn't speak for the entire ride to the hospital. He spoke curtly to the duty nurse, giving Molly's information right before the paramedics came in behind them, expediting the process. He held her hand when they checked her for concussion and waited patiently while they took her for x-rays. Molly *felt* his relief when the doctor told them her arm wasn't broken, just badly bruised. He insisted on putting it in a sling so she wouldn't be tempted to move it. Sam took the prescription from the doctor and filled it for her while she waited.

By the time they were back in his truck, where he'd insisted on buckling her in himself, Molly was more concerned about him than her arm. As he started the vehicle, she reached out with her good arm and put a hand on his leg. His fingers clenched on the steering wheel and his head turned in her direction. Anxiety roiled in her stomach like a ship in a storm.

"Are you…are you okay?"

He shook his head, looked out the window and then back at her again. Her heart dropped into her stomach at his expression.

"It was terrifying. Knowing you were in that car. Following you with absolutely no control over what would happen. Thinking, when I finally got to the car that you wouldn't be okay."

Molly bit her lip. She hadn't purposely walked into the situation, but she couldn't deny that this wasn't the first time she'd caused him concern. Sam unbuckled and turned in his seat, staring at her with an unreadable expression.

"I didn't know. When I got in, I didn't know it was her," she whispered.

Sam closed his eyes as if he were the one in pain. When he opened them, the intensity of his gaze trapping the air in her lungs, creating pressure.

"I shouldn't have let you go. You're so independent and I've never been an alpha sort of guy, you know? I think you're amazing. You're the strongest woman I've ever met and that's saying something because you've seen how strong my mother is. I've never had this…this…overwhelming desire to protect someone. Someone who doesn't want to be protected and that makes me feel helpless."

Tears pricked Molly's eyes and she stuck her tongue to the roof of her mouth in an effort to keep them at bay. It was not the first time she'd been told she was a lot to handle by a man. She was independent and adventurous and she liked to keep busy. She wasn't afraid to explore or walk into the unknown. She never intended to be reckless and she could happily do without the near-death situation she'd found herself in twice now, but that didn't mean she could change who she was.

You just survived a car wreck with an off-her-rocker crazy woman. You can handle this. Cry later.

"I understand if…" she stopped. No, she didn't. She didn't understand.

"If what?" His brows furrowed.

Taking a deep breath, ignoring the pain in her ribs and in so many other places on her body, she looked out the window.

"If this is too much for you. My life has hardly been quiet or serene in the last few months. Though I hardly think it's my fault." She couldn't keep the bitterness from her voice.

There was a pull-down arm rest between them. She didn't look when he pushed it up and slid across the seat. She didn't think she could handle looking into his eyes as he confirmed her thoughts.

With a gentleness that washed over her like the warmth of the sun, Sam touched his fingers to her chin and turned her face to his. Molly swallowed the lump in her throat only to have another take its place.

"You think you're too much for me? You think I want to break up with you?" His words were a harsh whisper. His eyes were like fire pressing into her skin.

"Don't you?"

"No." He shook his head as if he couldn't believe what she'd said. His hand cupped her cheek and he pressed his forehead to hers, like he was trying to become a part of her. "I don't want to break up with you. I want to wrap you in my arms and keep you so close to me that you can't breathe without me feeling it. I want to protect you and keep you safe and I just let you go. *I just let you go with her* and it could have cost you your life. As soon as you walked out the door, I felt like something was wrong and by the time I came out of the bakery, you were gone. And all I could do was watch you go. I don't know how to take care of you and worse, I don't think you want me to. But watching you go, watching the car swerving, knowing you were in it, I realized that I'd never be able to forgive myself if I lost you."

Her breath came out closer to a sob. She covered his hand with hers. "It's not your fault. It's no one's fault. And I'm right here. I'm okay."

His eyes closed again as he whispered, "I'm not sure if I am yet."

He pulled back and pressed his mouth to hers. "I can't believe you thought I was breaking up with you."

One side of her lips quirked up. "I feel like I'm a little high maintenance lately."

Sam's laughter filled the cab. "Good thing maintenance is my specialty."

He pulled her close without jarring her arm and as his lips touched the outer edge of her ear, he whispered, "I'm not going anywhere."

Some of the tears escaped and she gripped his shirt in her fist. "Me neither."

There were a lot of things Molly wasn't sure about: the why and how of Skyler's death, if everyone else was okay, what would happen to Kyle. *But this,* she thought as she breathed him in, *of this, I'm sure.*

* * * *

What looked like a thousand mini mason jars lit with votive candles lined the stairs Molly used every day to get to the beach. They flickered in the soft breeze coming off of the water, but held their glow thanks to the higher edges of the jar. Instrumental music played softly from a Bluetooth speaker. Molly and Sam walked hand in hand. He kept sneaking glances at her to make sure she was okay. Smiling at him, she squeezed his fingers. She was bruised and stiff and it would be worse tomorrow, but she wasn't missing this. The sand was soft under their feet as they made their way toward the very small crowd that included Patricia, Katherine, Sheriff Saron, and a few people Molly didn't recognize. Ahead of them, at the base of the stairs, a man who Molly assumed was the minister stood in a dark gray suit. He smiled at them a moment before Molly caught movement coming down the stairs.

Her eyes locked on Chantel's and she held her breath as the woman looked at the scene before her. She and Blake stopped about a quarter way from the bottom, their hands clasped.

"What is all this?" Blake asked, staring at Patricia.

Chantel pressed a hand to her mouth and shook her head slowly. "It's our wedding."

Patricia stepped forward and the minister stepped to the side. Standing in a semi-circle near the stairs, it was difficult not to overhear them.

"I want you to be happy. I may have gone about it the wrong way, but it's all that really matters. I'm so sorry about everything that's happened." Patricia gestured to the small gathering, giving a tight smile to Katherine and Molly in particular.

"These people helped us arrange this and if you're okay with it, I'd truly love to watch my little girl get married."

Chantel released Blake's hand and came down the last few steps to embrace her mom. She spoke into Patricia's hair, the sound muffled, but Molly was pretty sure she'd seen the shine of tears. A moment later she stepped back, nodded, and blasted Molly with a smile she'd yet to show until now. Patricia held out a hand to Blake and he came closer, kissed her cheek. Then the two of them stood on the third stair as the minister married them. The sun ducked down behind the far-off mountains, leaving traces of red and orange and pink. Sam squeezed Molly's hand and with exquisite care, slipped his arm around her waist and tucked her close to his side.

Sheriff Saron's fingers linked with Katherine's, as Patricia sniffled into a handkerchief, a quiet contentment shining in her smile. It absolutely wasn't perfect. How could it have been with the events of the past few days? But at that moment, none of that touched the happy couple. They vowed to honor and love each other, to stand by one another's side through all of life's trials and tribulations. Blake gazed adoringly down at Chantel as they held each other's hands, repeating the minister's words softly, never once losing their smiles. Bad things would still happen and hard times would add pressure to the life they built together, but through it all, they promised to hang on tight and weather the storm together. It was all anyone could hope for.

Molly looked up at Sam and he turned his gaze on hers. No one knew what the next day might bring, but knowing there was someone who wanted to be yours, who wanted you to be theirs regardless of what unfolded, was a precious gift that Molly silently vowed to never take for granted.

When the minister announced that the groom could kiss his bride, he did so happily and they all clapped. They didn't stick around, but Molly felt like one day, they might be back. She hoped that Britton Bay didn't hold only bad memories for them. Working together, the guests cleaned up the small spot on the beach and within minutes, it was like the wedding had never happened. But the happy glow of the ceremony and the happily ever after

Blake and Chantel secured for themselves, gave Molly unexpected closure. There were still questions, but she only needed one answered tonight.

Catching Katherine's eye as they strolled back to their vehicles, Molly peered around Sam. "Is there still cake at the house?"

Sam, Katherine, and Sheriff Saron laughed, the sound rolling over the water and lifting into the air.

"Yes. There's lots of cake. And I say, we eat it all," Katherine said.

Chapter Twenty-Five

Molly wasn't sure why she was nervous. The police station was becoming a second home to her and now, she was sure, the real killer was in custody. Still, as she and Sam walked through the lobby, their footsteps echoing on the linoleum, she shivered. Sam looked her way.

"You all right?"

"Yeah. I just wish I'd pieced it together earlier," she replied.

"I don't know how you pieced any of it together. I've gotta say, I would be totally on board if you wanted to take up a new hobby. Maybe surfing or motor cross. Something safer than figuring out murders."

Molly released his hand to poke him in the side. "Very funny. I don't seek out the drama."

He smiled at her. "I know. It finds you."

"Hey, guys. How are you doing, Molly?" Priscilla asked as she approached the counter with a stack of files in her hands. She set them down and leaned on the countertop.

"I'm good. It's just bruised," Molly said, referring to her arm, which was still in a sling for a few more days until the swelling went down.

"I heard the bride and groom got hitched after all," Priscilla said.

"They did. I'm glad they were able to," Molly answered, feeling unusually antsy.

"Because of you," Sam said quietly beside her.

"Molly. Sam," Chris said, coming out of one of the offices.

Priscilla pressed the buzzer so they could come through the gate.

"Hey," Sam greeted with ease.

Molly gave a small wave. She'd come to give her statement, but hoped she wasn't getting a lecture.

"Come on back. How are you, Molly? Doc said the elbow isn't broken," Chris said, leading them into one of the interrogation rooms. She wondered if Kyle and Shannon had both been questioned in this very space.

"It's not. Just sore. I'm fine." She looked around the nondescript room that held a table, four chairs, and a mirror that she suspected was also a window from the other side.

Sam held her chair out for her and she slipped into it, grateful when he scooted a chair closer and took it, putting a comforting hand on her knee.

Chris sighed heavily as he sank into a chair across from them. "This one threw more curveballs than a game going into double overtime."

"She was so angry," Molly said quietly. She hadn't allowed herself to think much about it over the last day and a half.

Sam's fingers tightened on her leg. Chris's mouth tightened into a firm line.

"I'm sorry we let it get that far and very grateful you're okay," he said.

"You and me both," Sam said.

The two men held each other's gaze and Molly put her hand over Sam's. "It's no one's fault."

"That's not entirely true," Chris said, a hard edge to his voice.

Shannon's words came back to her. "She said Skyler stole her recipe. The one that cinched the contest for her. She took the winnings and the credit."

"How long were you in the car before you realized?" Chris asked. He didn't pick up the pen to scrawl anything on the paper. He just stared at her intently, a touch of the guilt she'd seen in Sam's eyes shadowing his.

"When I saw her tattoo again. I'd seen it once before, when you arrested Kyle. It didn't click then, but Corky must have seen Shannon leaving Skyler's room because when I saw him on the morning of her death, he kept talking about the dark stars. I shouldn't have just walked away when he was so upset." She looked at Sam and gestured to her shoulder. "Shannon has a line of small, black stars tattooed on her shoulder."

He just shook his head, renewed anger furrowing his brow. She wanted to smooth it with her fingers.

"We didn't pay much attention to Corky either. He hasn't been the same since. He's actually staying at the shelter just outside of town, which is a big step forward."

"He must have been so scared," Molly said, thinking of the way he'd wrung his hands together. "How did you know it wasn't Kyle? Because of the coffee? Skyler's DNA wasn't on the lid, was it?"

Chris's eyes widened. "Excuse me?"

Sam straightened, but didn't say anything.

Molly took a deep breath and shared what she had manage to put together. "I knew Skyler had been poisoned, but she never drank or ate anything that she hadn't prepared herself. It was a self-preservation rule because she had so many allergies."

"How is it you know about her allergies?" Chris crossed his arms over his chest and leaned back in his seat.

"Uh, I was told? By more than one...source. Anyway, I knew she wouldn't drink anything that she didn't make so there was no way, even if Bella had brought her a latte, it was her. Which meant it must have been Kyle and since he wasn't dead, that couldn't have been the source of the poison. It had to be something that she trusted. Something Shannon could access without making her suspicious." There was something she was missing. What else had she learned that morning?

Something Skyler would have trusted without hesitation. Not a drink. Not food. *Just brushing her teeth and then she fell.* Molly gasped and both men went on alert.

"What's wrong? Are you okay? Are you in pain?" Sam put a hand to her arm.

"What is it?" Chris leaned forward.

"Corky said Skyler was brushing her teeth."

Chris closed his eyes and exhaled heavily. When he opened them, the frustration in his gaze turned her stomach. "We found traces of sesame oil on her toothbrush. It was one of a long list of ingredients that could put her into anaphylactic shock."

Molly's stomach cramped. "She said it was only supposed to make her sick. Not kill her. She must have visited her after Kyle left. They broke up that night. Maybe Shannon visited under the guise of consoling her. Even though I don't think there was any real friendship between them, ever."

"Whatever the reason, Skyler let her in and it wouldn't have taken much to gain access to the bathroom. She put it directly on the toothbrush. The tube of toothpaste was untouched, but we found Shannon's prints on the toothbrush."

"It's so sad," Molly said. "All of this for what? Some prize money and recognition?"

"Unfortunately, people kill for less. I'm just very glad that the collateral damage on this one didn't go any further than it did."

"It very nearly did." Sam's tone betrayed his simmering anger.

"But everything is okay. Mostly. I mean, someone still died." There was no getting around that and definitely no getting used to it. Molly could happily live the rest of her life without being anywhere near another death.

"I think it's important that you realize how close you came to getting hurt," Chris said.

And here comes the lecture. She gestured to her arm. "Pretty clear on it."

"Maybe you should have taken some of her concerns more seriously," Sam said.

Chris stiffened. "Now hang on."

"Boys, don't." She looked at Sam.

The fierce affection in his gaze warmed her, made her wish they were curled up on one of their couches rather than in this sterile room.

"I don't want you getting involved in this kind of stuff either, but the bottom line is, yeah, it's not ideal to have citizens involved in any way, but this town is too small for the people who live here not to see and hear things that can be helpful to you guys."

"We take all information and tips seriously, Sam. And I value the information you've given us, Molly, but you have to understand that we're here to protect the citizens and that's harder to do when they're dead set on solving mysteries just because they seem appealing."

"Hey!" Now Molly stiffened.

"I can't help it if I stumbled onto information. I did not actively pursue anything other than an interview." Maybe that wasn't all the way true, but she really hadn't gone looking for trouble.

"I know that things don't move as fast as anyone would like. We're a small department doing the best we can. On a personal level, I care about what happens to you, Molly. Because you're clearly important to one of my best friends. I don't want to be the guy in charge if something happens to you. That's all. I'm not trying to lay blame or anything."

"He just knows that if he is the guy in charge one day, and something happens under his watch, I'll beat him up."

Molly laughed, happy the tension receded that easily.

"You wish," Chris said, smirking.

"You know what we need?" Molly said, looking at Sam.

"I know what I'd like," he said, his eyes heating in a way that made her heart tremble. "But if I'm inside your adorable brain...I'm guessing you're thinking about food."

Molly laughed. "Good guess."

"I'm about to wrap up here. I do need you to write your statement, but Shannon has been transferred to a county prison. I can save the rest of the paperwork until tomorrow. Why don't I call Sarah and we'll meet you at Come 'n Get It?" Chris looked back and forth between them.

"That sounds extremely...normal. I'm in," Molly said.

"Me too. We'll grab a table and meet you there."

Chris slid the notepad toward Molly. "I just need to know what happened in the few minutes you were in the car. We have everything else." He stood up. "I'll be back. I'm just going to call Sarah."

When he left, Molly picked up the pen and started to write. She felt Sam's gaze on her and stopped, turned to face him.

"What is it?"

"It doesn't seem to matter if we're heading out for dinner, wrapped up in each other, or sitting at a police station, you make me happy."

She set the pen down and put her hand to his cheek, her heart too full for her chest. "I've been a little scared to feel everything I do for you. But it appears I have no choice."

He nodded, giving her an adorable grin. "I am pretty convincing."

"Yes, you are," she laughed, leaning in for a kiss. "Now let me fill this out so we can eat."

"See? Right back to making me happy," Sam said, once again, making her grateful she'd taken a chance on Britton Bay. And them.

When they left, a short while later, Sam stared at her across the cab of his truck.

"So what now?" he asked, picking up her hand. Neither of them were in a rush to get into the diner.

"Now?"

"Yeah. You going to be okay when everything goes back to normal? You haven't really experienced our town at its quietest."

Molly smiled. "Trust me, I'm looking forward to it." She thought of all the things that had happened in just a few days and it created a dizzy feeling in her brain. "A little quiet and a lot of normal sounds perfect to me."

He leaned over, kissed the side of her head, breathing her in.

"Although, it occurs to me, there's one thing I would like to do," Molly said, unhooking her seat belt.

Sam did the same. "Should I be worried?"

She laughed, and waited until he came around the vehicle to take her hand once they'd gotten out.

"I kept thinking that a great way to get information would be a girls' night."

"You don't need information anymore."

She looked up at him. "Exactly. So maybe I should focus on just making some friends."

His gaze softened, turning tender. "That's a good idea. Friends keep you...grounded. Rooted to a place."

Happiness washed over her and she stepped closer to him, wrapped her good arm around his neck. His arms looped around her waist. "I don't need friends for that. I like it here. More than I ever thought possible. I'm not going anywhere."

Sam's forehead touched hers. "I like the sound of that."

"Good," she whispered, brushing her mouth against his, right there in the middle of the sidewalk on Main Street. "Because it's true."

Please turn the page for an exciting sneak peek of
Jody Holford's next Britton Bay mystery
DEADLY RIDE
Coming soon!

Chapter One

Molly Owens had a pretty strong grasp on vocabulary, but clearly, she misunderstood the word chilly. When the locals, including her boyfriend, told her that the seaside town she'd taken up residence in would start getting *chilly* at the beginning of October, she wasn't concerned. As a former army brat, she'd lived all over and had known cold. She'd seen snow. Maybe she didn't remember it all that well, but she had survived low temperatures. Though her brain must have blocked it out like a traumatic memory.

When she stepped outside of the little cottage she rented behind a bed-and-breakfast, a gust of wind kicked up its heels and danced over every inch of her body. Her dog, a sweet little black and white fur ball, tugged on his leash, undaunted by the frigid air. He was ready for his morning walk by the beach whether she was or not.

"Oh. My. Goodness." She barely stopped her teeth from chattering. Chilly was 'Grab a sweater for later when the sun goes down'. *This,* was 'Where did I put my parka and earmuffs?' weather. Britton Bay, Oregon was not simply *chilly.*

"It's freezing," she said to Tigger, who continued to tug. Wishing she had gloves, but really wanting to get the walk in, she tugged the sleeves of her jacket down, trying to warm her hands.

Tigger plodded forward, knowing the route from their cottage to the ocean front.

She laughed through the shivers. "Okay, okay. Calm down. How are you not cold?"

Giving a bark of enthusiasm, Tigger led the way with his nose, sniffing at every inch of the same path they took daily. Molly looked over to the two story Victorian home. It's gorgeous, soft blue coloring made it blend with the sky on a perfect day. No one was on the back porch today. *Too cold out.* Anyone smart would have stayed tucked under the covers.

Molly smiled when she thought of the man tucked under her covers. The one who sleepily asked if she'd wanted company for the walk, falling back asleep before she could reply. For someone who ran his own business, one that often saw early clientele, Sam did not enjoy early mornings.

Before coming to Britton Bay, Molly hadn't cared one way or the other. She got up for work each day when she'd lived in L.A. Routine and repetition ground out having a preference. Since coming to this little dot of a town on the Oregon coast though, seeing the sun rise over the water had become addictive.

She and Tigger crossed the quiet road and headed into the thicket of trees that parted only enough to create a walkable path. She'd found the short cut to the beach her first week here. Which was just over five months ago now. *Almost half a year. Where did the time go?* Tigger stopped to investigate what he must have felt was a particularly aromatic path of flowers. The colorful petals were tipped with ice. The wind was getting stronger now that they were closer to the beach.

"Come on, you." She tugged him toward the rough, pine steps that led down to the water. She could hear it weaving back and forth, even through the trees. Increasing her pace, she all but jogged down the steps. It was only *just* October now and they'd had a run of warm, sunny days to close out September. Hopefully, they'd get a few more before winter actually hit.

At the end of the steps, Molly's feet sank into the sand. She pulled in as much fresh air as she could and despite the *chill,* her smile widened. The sky was a blurry wash of shades: red, orange, and yellow merging and overlapping. The water, deceptively still, shone with the reflection of cloud puffs and color.

Tigger sat on her feet, his favorite spot, and whined, looking up at her. She crouched down and rubbed his side, laughing when he nudged her with his nose.

"Worth the chill and the early hour, huh, boy?"

He yipped at her then lowered the front of his body, wagging his tail with endless enthusiasm. As they walked along the beach, her reveling in the quiet and him reveling in the scents, she thought being here, in Britton Bay, was worth a lot of things.

It was worth the long, roundabout way she'd gotten here. It was strange to think, but sometimes she felt like this little pocket of the earth had been waiting for her to show up and start her life. From the moment she'd arrived, she breathed better, her pulse slowed, and she'd found something she hadn't in all of the other places she'd tried to settle: contentment.

As they scooted up the curve of the beach, taking the walking path up to the pier, Molly saw Bella, who owned Morning Muffins, working on her sidewalk chalkboard sign. Using a bright yellow piece of chalk, Molly watched her make the shape of an "L" and grinned.

"Please say that's the start of you telling the world your lemon loaf is the special today." Molly pulled Tigger back when he started to prance forward on his back paws in his eagerness to see the baker.

Bella's musical laughter filled the air and she looked up at Molly. "It's like you're a mind reader. Or sign reader, I guess. Hello, Tigger. Are you ever not happy, bud?" Setting the chalk down, she pet him and laughed again when he went belly up.

Molly couldn't help but laugh at her pup's shameless bid for as much attention as possible.

"You guys are out earlier than usual," Bella said, returning to her lettering.

Molly crouched and got Tigger to sit with a little more dignity at her side. "I like to be at the paper early on Thursdays but didn't want to miss out on the walk. I don't think I'll ever get tired of the view."

"It's something," Bella agreed. She made a loop for the second 'L' then glanced over at Molly. "Sam excited about the car show?"

"He is. Stressed, I think, though he wears it well. But it's the first time I've seen him make an actual to-do list." Sam's auto shop was hosting and sponsoring the event and her evenly keeled boyfriend revealed nerves only in the subtlest of ways.

Standing and shaking the cramp out of her legs, she checked her phone and wondered if he was out of bed yet. They both needed to get to their respective jobs.

"It's so nice that we have one more event to look forward to before the town really shuts down for winter," Bella said.

"It is. The official start is tomorrow, but the event organizers are arriving today. Jill is heading over to Come 'n Get It this evening to interview them."

Bella smiled as she stood up and wiped her hands on her apron. A few years younger than Molly, the baker never wore makeup and always had her hair tucked up in one of those buns that looked prettily messed. Today was no exception.

"I love that Jill is back in town. It's almost like she never left," Bella said. In typical small-town fashion, Jill was Sam's cousin and a good friend of everyone's favorite baker. The connections among its residents were endless, but Molly realized she didn't feel like an outsider anymore.

"I heard you're offering a decorating class during the festival." It was one of the many family friendly activities being offered during the almost three-day event.

"I am. For kids. I thought it would be a unique way to showcase my food, but also help out with things for them to do. My dad used to drag me to car shows when I was a kid and all I can ever remember thinking was how boring they were." Bella picked up her chalk and tucked it back in the box.

"I've never been to one," Molly admitted. She'd never had a reason.

Bella glanced at the time through her shop window. "You want some lemon loaf? I need to open up."

"I absolutely do," Molly said. Tigger wagged his tail at the pitch of her voice.

Bella laughed and bent to pet him again. "I think I might have a dog bone for you, mister. Be right back."

Lemon loaf in hand, pup leading the way, Molly was wide awake by the time she got back to her cottage. She loved it here. Really and truly loved it. Her little house was tucked between evergreens, looking like it had sprouted naturally at the back of the property. It was a one bedroom with its own miniature front garden and a big enough fenced back area for Tigger to run around.

Thinking she'd need to wake Sam up without the temptation of crawling back into bed with him, she was surprised to hear him moving around in the kitchen. She took the leash off of Tigger and hung it, removing her shoes while the dog made a mad dash. She walked into the kitchen to the sound of Sam's laughter and her heart flip-flopped along with her stomach. How could just his laugh brighten her day?

She inhaled sharply, seeing that he was still wearing just flannel, checkered pajama bottoms. The smooth skin of his back and biceps, the disheveled state of his hair, and the way he grinned down at her dog was enough to make her mouth water. Yeah, she was definitely in the right place. As someone who was used to moving on, it was interesting to feel such a strong pull to stay.

The tattoo on his shoulder drew her attention, even as he turned, those gorgeous brown eyes zeroed in on her.

"Good morning," he said, his voice a little rough.

A shiver raced over her skin and it had nothing to do with the weather. She walked to him, set the baked goods on the counter in front of him and wrapped her arms around his waist. His came around her as though they belonged there and she held on, breathing in his clean, crisp scent, which was more intoxicating than the ocean's.

"Morning. I wasn't sure you'd be up." She leaned back, accepted the sweet, gentle kiss he gave.

Her hand moved up his arm and she traced her fingers over the ink that he'd recently explained the meaning of. She'd wondered about the date, written in roman numerals inside of a vintage Route 66 sign.

"Your dad probably would have loved knowing you brought the Classic Car Crawl here to Britton Bay," she said. He'd started his auto repair shop using money from his father's life insurance after his passing. Sam spoke of his dad with so much love and respect, Molly was sorry she never got the chance to meet him.

"He would have. He took me to my first one in Las Vegas when I was nine. My mom was mad. Didn't think he should be taking me anywhere near The Strip. But once we got there, all we did was look at cars and I couldn't get enough." His hands sifted through her hair.

"Jethro and Brian will be getting into town later today," she said, referring to the Classic Car Crawl founders. "Do you know if they're staying at the hotel?" Sam's mom, Katherine, ran the bed-and-breakfast and hadn't mentioned it.

"Nah. They're staying at the RV park. They both pull their cars behind them when they travel."

Molly scrunched her nose up. "I don't think I'd like knowing that much was behind me when I drove."

Sam grinned. "They've been doing this for over twenty years, driving state to state. They're used to it. And when I say RV, I mean miniature luxury home."

"I think I'm happier with just my Jeep. Unless you want to go camping some time, then I think I could handle hauling a tent. Though, I'd rather stay at the bed-and-breakfast than in either of those."

When he picked up a strand of her hair and played with it between his fingertips, she was momentarily distracted. He was always touching her, like he was part of her and she was starting to get used to the feeling.

"I have to go. I was thinking I could bring you over some lunch later. You'll be busy. I don't want you to forget to eat."

Sam tugged her closer. "You taking care of me?"

The idea sent a warm feeling through her body, starting at her chest and moving all the way down to her toes. "That okay?"

Pressing his forehead to hers, he closed his eyes, then opened them and pressed a kiss to the top of her head.

Tigger flopped between them, on both of their feet.

Sam looked down. "Hey, buddy. Am I hogging all of the attention?"

Molly laughed and hugged him tight. "He got plenty of attention. From me and from Bella. By the way, your description of October weather was drastically understated."

He let her go and picked up the brown bag on the counter, opening it. "Cold out there? I don't doubt it. Even when the sun is shining, it's like a switch is flipped, bringing out the frost."

Pulling out a piece of lemon loaf, he took a bite. "Mmm. I could start every morning like this."

Molly grabbed a plate from the cupboard for her own piece. "With Bella's baked goods?"

He poked her side with his index finger, then snaked his hand around her waist and pulled her to his side, kissing her temple. "I meant waking up to have you *bringing* me lemon loaf."

Her heart trembled. She'd lived with a man before and it had ended badly. Though she'd been careful to guard her heart with Sam, he'd easily snuck through all the barriers and if she wasn't cautious, she'd ignore all of her previously learned lessons and forget about taking it slow. The truth was, she'd love to wake up next to him every day. But the truth was also that they'd only been together less than six months.

Taking the second piece of lemon loaf out of the bag, she grinned at him. "Maybe we can buy it in bulk and freeze it," she suggested.

"Right," he said around another bite. "Except that you're equally addicted to Bella's scones and muffins so we'd also have to keep those on hand."

He wasn't wrong and the immediate lurch of her heart settled, her pulse returning to normal. There was nothing wrong with enjoying the little things with Sam—like bringing him lemon loaf after a freezing morning walk. She could think about the future and know he wanted to be in it without second guessing the thought. She'd never known anyone as loyal and innately kind as Sam. Other than his mother, Katherine, who ran the bed-and-breakfast and had happily welcomed her not only into the cottage, but into her family.

"You look too serious for not even seven a.m. You okay?"

Taking a small bite of the delicious lemon cake, she nodded. "I am. More than okay."

He reached out and stroked a hand down her hair. "Agreed. I need to shower and get to work. We on for later tonight?"

"Yup. Unless you get busy with stuff. But I can help if you need anything." She liked planning their day together.

Sam's smile chased away any residual chill from the morning. He stepped into her and kissed her again, before pulling her tight and burying his nose in her neck. When he pulled back, he kissed the tip of her nose.

"You should probably be careful, Molly Owens," he said with mock seriousness.

"Why's that?" She had to crane her neck to look up at him.

"Breakfast, lunch, and dinner with you? A guy could get pretty addicted to that."

Her heart nearly danced right out of her chest. *See? Not alone in how you feel.* And since he was so free with his affection and feelings, she could be as well.

Going up on tiptoe, she kissed him, just a gentle brush of her lips across his. "I think I'm okay with that."

When he grinned, gave Tigger an extra rub and then went to shower, Molly finished her lemon loaf with a grin on her face.

So much to look forward to. After a shaky end to the summer, Britton Bay was settling down again and Molly was settling right along with it. The car show would be driving into town tomorrow and she was excited to share in the town's enthusiasm, and mostly, in Sam's. This was a big event for him. A big deal for his business. Molly couldn't wait to stand by his side as he pulled off one of his dreams.